Holden's Promise

The *Emerson Moore* Adventures by Bob Adamov

- *Rainbow's End* — Released October 2002
- *Pierce the Veil* — Released May 2004
- *When Rainbows Walk* — Released June 2005
- *Promised Land* — Released July 2006
- *The Other Side of Hell* — Released June 2008
- *Tan Lines* — Released June 2010
- *Sandustee* — Released March 2013
- *Zenobia* — Released May 2014
- *Missing* — Released April 2015
- *Golden Torpedo* — Released July 2017
- *Chincoteague Calm* — Released April 2018
- *Flight* — Released May 2019
- *Assateague Dark* — Released May 2020
- *Sunset Blues* — Released May 2022
- *White Spider Night* — Released July 2022
- *Rainbow's End 20th Anniversary Edition* — Released October 2022
- *Sawdust Joint* — Released July 2023

The *Zeke Layne* Adventure by Bob Adamov

Memory Layne — Released May 2021

Next *George Ivers* Adventure:
Alone at Home

Holden's Promise

Bob Adamov

Packard Island Publishing
Wooster, Ohio
2024
www.packardislandpublishing.com
www.bobadamov.com

Copyright 2024 by Bob Adamov
All rights reserved.
No part of this book may be used or reproduced in any manner whatsoever without written permission from the author except in the case of brief quotations embodied in critical articles or reviews.

www.BobAdamov.com

This book is a work of fiction. Names, characters, places and incidents are either products of the author's imagination or are used fictitiously. Any resemblance to actual events, locales or persons, living or dead, is entirely coincidental.

First edition • March 2024

ISBN: 979-8-9853593-7-4

Printed and bound in the United States of America

Cover Art/Layout by: Ryan Sigler
Blue River Digital
303 Towerview Dr.
Columbia City, IN 46725
www.blueriverd.com

Published by:
Packard Island Publishing
3025 Evergreen Drive
Wooster, OH 44691
packardislandpublishing.com

Praise, Reviews and Awards for Bob Adamov's Novels

"… Adamov is a superb craftsman of hanging-on-the-edge-of-your-seat mystery adventures…" – Midwest Book Review

"… Adamov's natural flair for originality and a narrative storytelling style that is laced with unexpected plot twists and turns that will keep and hold the reader's fully entertained and rapt attention from cover to cover!" – Midwest Book Review

Adamov Voted **2022 Best Lake Erie Author** – Lake Erie Living magazine

*"One of **PublishOhio's Favorite Authors**"* – PublishOhio.com

*"Memory Layne Named **Best Fiction Novel** and **Action Adventure Finalist**"* – 2022 Next Generation Indie Awards

"A Great Read!" – Clive Cussler

"…Enough action to satiate James Bond fans…" – Lansing State Journal

"Memory Layne reminds me of Nicholas Sparks' The Notebook!" – Charles Meier, Key West author and star of the Science Channel's The Curse of The Bermuda Triangle

" Great Local Book!" – Eastern Shore of Virginia Tourism

"This book is like slipping on a pair of broken-in boat moccasins – comfortable and familiar." – Cleveland Magazine

*"**Honorable Mention**"* – Great Midwest, Florida, Hollywood, New York & London Book Festivals

"One of the best novels in northeast Ohio!" – Akron Beacon Journal

"…Fascinating tale of corporate greed, violence, and betrayal …" – Sun Newspapers

"This series is a must read for any diver or Clive Cussler fan! – Visibility Divers' Magazine

*"**2003 Great Lakes Book Award Finalist**"* – Great Lakes Independent Booksellers Association

Dedication

Holden's Promise is dedicated to Ryan and Rachel Ashley and their family: Judy, Chloe, Hannah and Hazel Harland. Ryan inspired this book when he posted a photo of a fish house on the banks of the Shallotte River on Facebook. That photo sparked the idea for a novel and resulted in a couple of research trips to Shallotte, N.C. and nearby Holden Island.

It's also dedicated to Barry, Fran, Corbett and Roddy Holden at the Holden Seafood Company who provided invaluable information about the area and their shrimp trawler.

They that wait upon the Lord shall renew their strength;
they shall mount up with wings as eagles;
they shall run, and not be weary;
and they shall walk, and not faint.
                 – **Isaiah 40:31**

Acknowledgments

After my friend Ryan Ashley moved from Wooster, Ohio to the Shallotte, North Carolina area and the Brunswick Islands, he posted on Facebook a picture of a seafood company building on the bank of a river. Seeing the picture birthed an idea for a novel set there. I made a few research trips to the area in 2023 where I was warmly welcomed and assisted by Ryan and Rachel Ashley, and Judy and Chloe Harland, his mother and sister. He introduced me to the Holden family who owned the Holden Seafood Company on Shallotte Point. Barry, Fran, Roddy and Corbett, who was engaged to Ryan's sister Hannah, were so kind in answering my questions and allowing me to interview them as well as tour their shrimp trawler.

When I stopped at Islands Art & Books in Ocean Isle Beach to purchase a colorful art print of shrimp trawlers, I met the gregarious gallery owner, Gary Pope. We just connected like we had known each other all of our lives. Of course, I had to put Gary and the gallery in this novel.

I also would like to acknowledge the assistance/coaching I received from South Carolina's famous shipwreck hunter Ralph Wilbanks and his wife Anne. Ralph discovered the Confederate submarine CSS *Hunley* in Charleston Harbor years ago. Ralph's unique style of southern humor and charm are so inspiring that I just had to include them in this adventure.

I'd like to thank my amazing senior editor John Wisse and my team of editors: Cathy Adamov and Michelle Marchese.

For more information, check these sites:
BobAdamov.com
VisitPut-in-Bay.com
MillerFerry.com

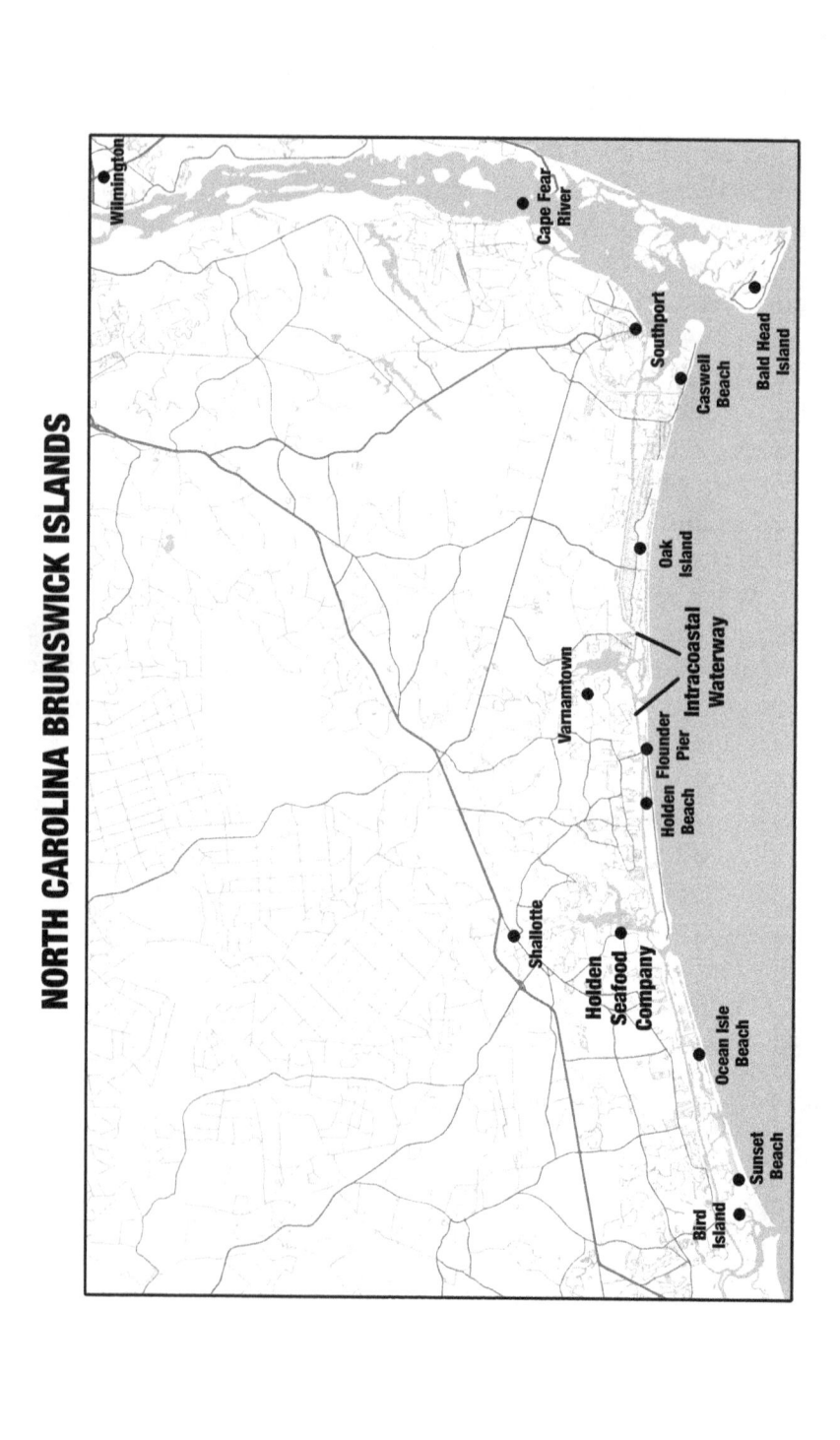

NORTH CAROLINA BRUNSWICK ISLANDS

Holden's Promise

Preface

Midevening
Off the North Carolina Coast

The rain-filled wind ruffled the captain's hair as he struggled to hold his hat securely on his head. He stood, rooted to the hurricane deck, as his mind weighed a number of factors. With narrowed eyes, he watched the two helmsmen as they fought the ship's wheel to maintain her course while heavy waves pummeled the struggling ship.

"Hard-a-starboard," Capt. Swafford rasped as the color drained from his rugged face. He coughed twice before cursing himself for not earlier taking shelter in a nearby port. His good sense was overridden by his determination to complete his mission to Wilmington. He wrestled with his decision, knowing his stubbornness could result in the loss of the steamer and its crew.

When the rudder came around, the ship shuddered heavily as she turned into the waves. As the torrential rain pounded the ship like bullets, Swafford felt the deck pitch forward while the ship maneuvered perceptibly slower to face into the wind and deadly seas. Coming around, there was one brief moment of relief from the battering waves. It was a false sense of relief as she rolled in the heavy swells with her decks awash from large volumes of seawater cascading over her sides.

The spinning behemoth wallowed in the heavy seas. Her bilge pumps could no longer keep up. The savage and unyielding wind howled as the violent stormy waves pressured the ironclad hull, threatening to separate the iron from its oak timbers.

Her bolts strained to hold the ship together from the relentless, powerful hammering of the waves.

The rapidly-moving hurricane with extremely dangerous winds of 120 m.p.h. caught the dark gray-painted, sidewheel steamer by surprise as she hugged the shoreline on her way to the port of Wilmington on the Cape Fear River. The CSS *Myrtle* rocked precariously in the deep troughs of the heavy seas as its coal-fired engines struggled to push the blockade runner through the downpour. Black smoke poured out of her two smokestacks as her hungry engines demanded more coal.

The ironclad vessel was 240-feet long with a beam of 26-feet. She drew a draft of 11-feet, and her low hull, which was just a few feet above the waterline, was driven by two side paddle wheels. Her cargo hold was filled with rifles and ammunition for the Confederate army.

Ship's captain William Swafford was thankful that earlier he had reacted quickly to the first swells of the sea as the darkened clouds dropped torrents of rain on his ship and crew. He had an ominous feeling that he needed to send the launch with the most precious of his cargo toward shore.

With its four double-banked oars dipping in the heavy seas and rising like the wings, the 29-foot launch pulled away from the floundering vessel. He had instructed his second-in-command to guide the craft to shore, and they would connect after the storm abated.

Reluctantly, the second-in-command complied. He preferred to stay aboard, but bowed to his captain's command. He slipped into the launch that was bobbing in the seas and scrambled to the tiller. Several crew members joined him and manned the oars as the salty spray covered them. They rowed away thirty minutes before the full fury of the storm struck the ship.

A shout from a crew member directed the captain's attention seaward where his eyes saw a towering wave at its pinnacle. The tsunami-like wave crashed over the steamer, swallowing it like a hungry sea monster and sending it to the bottom of the Atlantic as its boilers exploded. All hands were lost.

CHAPTER 1

Present Day
South Bass Island, Ohio

Perched on a limestone cliff on the southwest side of the island, the bow section of the freighter *Benson Ford* overlooked the western basin of Lake Erie. Its 62-foot long by 59-foot-wide superstructure, including the forecastle deck, was moved to the site in July, 1986. This island getaway vacation home included black walnut-paneled state rooms, five bedrooms, five full baths, a dining room, living room, reading room, galley, garage and a massive family room. The pilothouse atop the four-story structure offered a breathtaking view of spectacular sunsets and approaching lake storms.

The brilliant sunset that evening was the reason for the gathering of five men on the patio next to the shiphouse. The group included the Awesome Threesome, a group of island entrepreneurs. Shiphouse owner Bryan Kasper hosted Paul Jeris and Brad Ohlemacher, his world traveling buddies who were ready to fly off to exotic destinations at the drop of a hat. Also in attendance were legendary island entertainer Mike "Mad Dog" Adams and Emerson Moore, a *Washington Post* investigative reporter residing on the island's East Point with his aged aunt.

The jovial, white-haired Kasper was holding a bottle of his award-winning Shiphouse Vodka, a product from his distillery operation in the downtown island resort village of Put-in-Bay, the "Key West of the Midwest." The glass bottle was modeled in the shape of the *Benson Ford* shiphouse.

"Fill your glasses, gentlemen?" Kasper, who was the adventurous one, offered as he looked at the group known for their camaraderie and laughter-filled tales.

"Okay by me," Ohlemacher said as he tipped back the brim of his bright red cap. It was lettered boldly with the words "Joe's Bar," the local watering hole that he owned along with the Bird's Nest B & B.

"Like you had to ask?" the wily Adams chuckled.

As Kasper poured, the men watched the western sky. The sunset was painting an array of colors from orange to red to pink as it disappeared. It left a comforting silence filled with the rhythmic percussion of waves breaking on the limestone cliff and rocks below. A cool lake breeze blew a freshness through the early evening air.

"I think I could sit here all night," Moore commented appreciatively. "What a beautiful sunset," the tanned, dark-haired, fortyish reporter added.

"Nothing like them," Ohlemacher added. "As if we were in Key West."

Reluctantly, Moore glanced at his watch, then stood from his chair. "I'd love to stay, but I've got to catch the early ferry tomorrow morning," Moore explained.

"Where are you heading, Emerson?" Adams asked.

"Turkey? Saudi Arabia?" Jeris suggested, having traveled there in the past.

Jeris was heavily invested in the island with his ownership of several island taxi and golf cart companies. He was the property manager for 80 island homes and constructing new condos. He also managed the Put-in-Bay Island Guide and owned the Put-in-Bay.com website.

"I wish, although I've been to Turkey," Moore offered as he thought of a past adventure that took him to the southwest coast city of Bodrum.

"Istanbul?" Jeris asked.

"No, Bodrum. It's Europe's version of Put-in-Bay," Moore explained.

"Sounds more like Instant Bull to me," Adams quipped with a twinkle in his eyes.

"Seriously Mike, it is like party central for Europe. I even went to a club where they had a foam party," Moore countered.

"Beer foam?" Ohlemacher teased.

They all laughed.

"No. Nothing exciting like you guys do," Moore replied.

"I don't know about that, Emerson," Kasper began. "You have a reputation for taking off suddenly on your adventures."

"That's right," Jeris piped in with a sly grin.

"Not this time. I'm finally taking some time off. No adventures," Moore retorted.

"That will be the day," Adams spoke skeptically.

"I'm going on R & R in North Carolina. Need to relax while my ribs continue to heal," Moore said, thinking back to his recent adventure in Louisiana.

"You're welcome to join us on our next trip. You too, Mad Dog," Jeris offered.

Adams responded first. "I might take you up on that."

"Maybe. We'll see. But I really need to go," Moore concluded as he bid them farewell and walked over to his golf cart.

"One for the road?" Kasper asked as he held up the bottle of Shiphouse Vodka.

"Next time, Bryan," Moore called as he eased his six-foot-two frame on the golf cart and started its engine.

Within minutes, he was driving north along West Shore Boulevard. He turned right onto Portsmouth and made another right onto Bayview which took him along the waterfront. He followed it past the downtown docks and DeRivera Park. The downtown area of Put-in-Bay was crowded as the partying began. The restaurants and bars were filled with patrons looking to enjoy the evening activities.

Reaching his aunt's darkened house on East Point, Moore parked the golf cart in the garage and quietly entered it. His aunt must have gone to bed, he thought as he walked to the front porch where he saw boats in the nearby harbor rocking gently in a slight breeze.

He dropped in one of the white wicker chairs to enjoy the view and mindfully review his plans for the next day. Earlier he made arrangements to meet the owner of the Marblehead Soap Company on the mainland so he could buy soap for his hosts in North Carolina as a surprise gift.

Years ago, Moore had met Ryan Ashley in Washington, D.C. when he interviewed him about his black ops work in Iraq. The two had become good friends. Moore enjoyed watching his career as Ashley moved to Shallotte, North Carolina and started a successful construction business. He also assumed ownership of a restaurant on a pier in nearby Holden Beach which he remodeled. It was an excellent investment as business continued to flourish.

During a recent email exchange, Ashley invited Moore to spend some time with him and his wife, Rachel. Moore eagerly accepted as it had been a long time since he enjoyed a beach vacation free of any investigative work.

CHAPTER 2

The Next Morning
Marblehead Peninsula, Ohio

Moore had caught the Miller Ferry at Lime Kiln Dock for the short ferry ride to the Catawba Dock, followed by a brief drive over to the Marblehead Peninsula. He was looking forward to visiting the brick-faced store with its handcrafted organic soaps, honey, essential oils, candles and lake gifts. He parked his car across the street from the Marblehead Soap Company and crossed the street. As he pushed open the door to the store, he was greeted enthusiastically by its high-energy owner, Patti Wandover.

"Hi Emerson. Run out of soap already?" she asked with a broad smile as she walked over to the soap display. She picked up a bar of Peppermint Patti - Moore's favorite.

"I'm still good," he replied as he breathed in the rich fragrances of the store.

She held up another bar of soap. "I've got a new one here. It's called Grandma Farts," she giggled. "It goes along well with Grandpa Farts."

Moore chuckled softly. "I'm picking up a few items for friends of mine in North Carolina," he said as he wandered to the soap display.

"Off on another of your adventures, huh?" she asked bright-eyed.

"No. Not this time. It's rest and relaxation."

"Right. I've heard that before. Take your time," she said as she walked over to the production area.

Moore spent a few minutes looking through the soaps and

picked out several bars of Sounds Like a Midlife Crisis – Cigars and Motorcycles for Ryan and Pumpkin Crunch Cake for Ryan's wife. He picked up a large bottle of honey for himself. The honey came from the hives that Patti kept on her farm.

"All set?" she asked as he placed his items on the counter.

"That should do it," he affirmed as he allowed his eyes to gaze to the left side of the store where lake wear was displayed. His eyes stopped for a moment as he locked onto a series of Put-in-Bay mystery adventure books. "I see you carry Bob's books."

"I do. That guy is a character. Did you hear about his son wrapping his daughters in bubble wrap when Bob went to visit them? It was just after he babysat his grandson who ended up with a broken arm," she laughed.

"I didn't hear that one," Moore replied as he paid her for his purchase. "Sounds like a dangerous grandpa to me."

"That's for sure. Have a safe trip and be careful," she called as he departed. It seemed like everyone was telling him to be careful, Moore thought as he stepped into the car. He started the engine and began his two-day drive to Shallotte, North Carolina. He planned on driving until he was tired before checking into a motel.

Shallotte was located 33 miles southwest of Wilmington and 38 miles northwest of Myrtle Beach. The small town was nestled on the riverbank of the Shallotte River which years ago bustled with river traffic. It was about ten minutes inland from Holden Beach, Ocean Isle Beach and Sunset Beach.

Moore would be staying southeast of town on Shallotte Point on the banks of the Shallotte River. He was looking forward to relaxing on nearby Holden Beach, the 2.7-square mile barrier island bounded on one side by the Intracoastal Waterway and the Atlantic Ocean on the other side. The island was connected to the mainland by a towering 65-foot-high steel and concrete bridge measuring 1,800 feet long.

Holden Island's ownership dated to 1756 when it was purchased by Benjamin Holden. Later, the Holden family would acquire additional acreage and also start a commercial fishing business and a hotel on the island. They built a wooden bridge in 1925 to connect the island to the mainland, which subsequently was removed due to the construction of the Intracoastal Waterway. They eventually expanded into developing vacation homes on the island with a focus to make the island family-friendly – a focus that remained today.

CHAPTER 3

The Next Evening
Shallotte, North Carolina

Pulling off Route 17, Moore drove through Shallotte's business district filled with stores, gas stations and restaurants. He headed for the Ashley home on Bill Holden Road. He turned left off Village Pointe Road SW onto the tree-lined road. As he neared the end of the road, he spotted the Holden Seafood Company building on the bank of the Shallotte River. It had several outbuildings and a shrimp trawler that was rocking gently at the dock as the tide ran out.

He turned into the drive next to the seafood building. It led to a one-story, ranch style house with a screened-in porch. The front door opened, and a 40-year-old man with close-cropped, dark hair emerged. He was wearing rimless glasses and a big smile as he greeted his visitor.

"You made it!" Ryan Ashley could be heard exclaiming as he emerged from his porch. Moore exited his vehicle and strode toward Ashley. The two men then stood face to face and vigorously shook hands.

"I made good time – no accidents or detours," Moore announced. He then turned his attention to Ashley's bare arms and inquired, "Any more tattoos?"

"Not yet, but I'm thinking of a couple," he grinned. "If you're not tired from the drive, I'll take you over to the restaurant on Holden Island and you can say hello to the family."

Moore eyed the cobalt blue Honda Civic EX-T sedan and Suzuki SV650S motorcycle. "Which one?" he asked, knowing Ashley's love for speed.

"Neither. We're going by boat. Come on," he urged as he led Moore past the Holden Seafood Company building and onto the dock.

Glancing at the building, Moore asked, "The Holdens are related to you, right?"

"Yes. Corbett Holden is engaged to my sister, Hannah. He captains that trawler. Corbett's parents, Barry and Fran, run the seafood business, and his brother Roddy helps out. You'll like Roddy. He's the free spirit of the family. We always warn the ladies to watch out for him," Ashley teased.

"He sounds like an interesting and fun guy."

"He is. You'll get a chance to meet them all tomorrow. Maybe we can get you aboard the trawler to go shrimping."

"I'd like that." Moore saw the shrimp trawler as they walked along the dock. "Are we going to Holden Island on that shrimp trawler?" he asked skeptically, knowing that trawlers were not known for their speed.

"No silly. We're going in my boat," he said as he pointed at a center console Sea Hunt docked behind the trawler's stern. "The way the roads are laid out here, it's faster to take the boat than drive over to Holden Island."

"I like the name of your boat," Moore smiled as he glanced at the boat's stern. It read *My Rachel*.

"Not as much as my wife likes it," Ashley beamed.

"Smooth talker," Moore chided him good-naturedly.

The two men boarded the light blue, 2019 Sea Hunt Ultra 225 with a 200 HP Yamaha outboard motor. Moore released the lines while Ashley started it. Within seconds, the boat was moving downriver.

"We'll take the Shallotte River down to the Intracoastal Waterway, then take a left and go up to the bridge that connects the mainland to Holden Island. We'll dock below the bridge. It's a short walk from the foot of the bridge across the road to the restaurant."

"You've accomplished a lot since moving down here," Moore remarked.

"Yeah. Totally unexpected. My construction business exploded with new clients and projects. Then the opportunity came up for me to buy the restaurant on the pier. I couldn't pass it up."

Ten minutes later, they had docked below the island bridge.

As he stepped on the dock, Moore noticed out of the corner of his eye a movement in the water. He turned sharply to identify what it was, but didn't quite see it.

"I know what you think you saw and you're right," Ashley grinned.

"Shark?"

"Right. Sometimes you can see bull sharks swimming around the waterway and up the river. A lot of times, they'll give birth upriver," Ashley explained.

"Ryan, how big do the bull sharks get around here?"

"Seven to ten feet."

"I guess I won't be going swimming here," Moore commented warily.

"You don't see them around here often." Ashley pointed to a fish cleaning station overlooking the waterway. "Sometimes you'll see them swimming around there, waiting for fish scraps," Ashley added.

"I take chances, but I'm real careful around sharks."

"As you should be. I get on my kid sister Chloe all of the time. She'll take breaks from the restaurant and come down here to sit on the dock to dangle her feet in the water," Ashley stated.

"Kids!" Moore sighed.

"Yeah. There not like us, huh, Emerson? We never did anything risky as kids, right?" Ashley grinned.

"Of course not," Moore shot back with a smile.

"My mom is all over her about sticking her feet in the water," Ashley said as he led Moore away from the dock.

"There's the restaurant," Ashley said with pride as he pointed across Ocean Boulevard to the pier that extended out from the shore into the Atlantic Ocean. They walked through the full parking lot and up the steps to the wooden restaurant perched on top of the pier. The sign overhead announced Flounder Pier.

They paused at the entrance as Ashley commented, "We've got stunning views of Holden Beach and the Atlantic."

Moore nodded his head in agreement as he looked at the waves breaking on the sandy beach below and the darkening horizon.

"If you look back to where we docked, we offer our customers who sit in the west side of the restaurant free sunset views," Ashley cracked with a grin. "And if you're here early in the morning for breakfast, you can enjoy an amazing sunrise at no extra charge," he quipped.

"You're a real generous guy," Moore chuckled softly as Ashley held the door open for him to enter.

Stepping inside the wooden building, Moore found a crowded area with customers waiting for an empty table. His eyes quickly swept through the cozy and casual interior filled with diners seated at wooden tables and chairs with lanterns hanging from the beamed ceiling. The large indoor dining room was surrounded with large windows that were open so that the fresh sea breeze cooled the inside. There was a tropical tiki bar at the far end. The kitchen operations were in the middle of the restaurant.

"Nice view," Moore commented appreciatively as he gazed through the open windows.

"Incredible, isn't it? That's why the kitchen is in the middle. We wanted our customers to enjoy the waves crashing on the shore and the boats sailing by. They love it when a trawler comes in with a big flock of seagulls following it."

"Who's your friend, Ryan?" the blonde, teenage hostess asked.

"Chloe, this is Emerson Moore. He's going to be staying at my house for a week or so," Ashley explained. Turning to Moore, Ashley introduced the 14-year-old. "Emerson, meet my sister, Chloe. She helps out hostessing."

"Nice to meet you, Chloe," Moore said.

Chloe smiled and blushed softly as she took in the ruggedly handsome reporter. Flushed, she asked, "Can I show you to your table? Ryan has one reserved for the two of you."

Before Moore could respond, he felt two arms tightly encircle him from behind. As he turned to deal with the intruder, he smelled the perfume. It was that fragrance which stopped him from taking a swing at her. He was still edgy from his last adventure and needed to relax. He turned to see Ashley's wife who again gripped him in a bear hug.

"Emerson, it's so good to see you again," the tall, attractive brunette greeted Moore warmly.

"It has been a while," Moore agreed. "How have you been?"

"Just dandy. That man of mine keeps me busy," Rachel replied with a big smile. She threw a wink at her husband.

Moore turned to Ashley. "Ryan, I love your restaurant. Did you name it Flounder Pier because you know how much I enjoy flounder?" Moore joked.

Ashley started to respond, but Rachel interrupted him. "Actually, it was going to be Grouper Pier, but Ryan kept mistyping it on everything as Groper Pier."

"Wasn't one of my best moments," Ashley admitted.

"I think he did it on purpose," Rachel added as she glanced at her husband with a grin. "I told him we wouldn't get any customers with a name like that."

"So you compromised?" Moore asked with a twinkle in his eyes.

"Yes. I thought Flounder Pier would be safer," she admitted.

"Don't be too sure of that," Ashley teased.

"I've got one more person for you to meet," Ashley said as a spry, older woman walked over to them from the kitchen. "This beautiful woman is my mother, Judy Harland."

Moore shook her extended hand as she spoke, "What a son I have. I wouldn't trade him for anything."

Moore nodded. "He definitely is a charmer. I remember seeing his Facebook post about you. He was sitting behind a table on a sidewalk and the table had a big sign leaning up against it. It said 'I have the best Mom ever. Change my mind'."

"That's my boy," she smiled proudly as she reached over and playfully rubbed the top of Ashley's head.

"And no one's changed my mind!" Ashley added. "Chloe, why don't you show us to our table?"

"Are you two joining us?" Moore asked Rachel and Judy.

"We're headed back to the kitchen. We've got hungry customers," Rachel said as the two women walked away.

The two men followed Chloe to a table at the far end. It was close to the bar where a commotion was underway.

"Trouble?" Moore asked.

"I can handle it," Ashley noted as he walked to the bar where a surly, half-shaven senior was arguing with the bartender. "Is there a problem here?"

The bartender replied, "Neville wants another round, but I'm cutting him off. He isn't happy about it."

Ashley placed a hand on Neville's arm. He spoke calmly but assertively, "Neville, I need you to respect my employees. We've had this conversation before. When Ivan feels it's necessary to stop serving you, then it's time for you to pay your bill and leave. Let's not make matters worse and cause a scene."

Neville pulled his arm away. "I'll just take my business elsewhere," he slurred angrily.

"You say that all of the time. Here, I'll escort you to the door," Ashley said as he gently pushed the man toward the front door.

Seeing the interaction, Moore walked over to back up Ashley in case he needed it. He followed the two men to the hostess stand where Neville suddenly took a swing at Ashley. It was a mistake because Neville hadn't seen Ashley reach behind the hostess stand in anticipation of trouble.

Ashley brought his right hand around quickly in reaction to the missed punch and connected with the side of Neville's head. In his hand, he held a phone book. Neville tripped and fell to the floor. As his face filled with a stunned look, he glanced up at Ashley. "Ryan, why did you have to go and do that?" he groused as Moore and Ashley helped him to his feet.

"You shouldn't have taken a swing at me," Ashley replied. "Be glad that I wasn't using the New York City phone book, Neville. Now come on. Out you go."

Before Ashley put away the phone book, Moore's sharp eyes noticed the picture on the phone book cover. "Is that Corbett's trawler?" he asked.

"Good eyes. It is. The *Capt. C.L. Holde*n is the cover picture," Ashley acknowledged. "Roddy wanted to be the centerfold, but the phone company wouldn't agree," Ashley joked.

Moore snickered quietly as the two men walked Neville down the steps where a couple of taxis were parked. Ashley helped Neville into the back of the first taxi and paid the driver to take Neville home.

Moore looked at Ashley. "I gather you know this guy, and this has happened before?"

"Yes. Neville's a retired trawler captain. He lives on Shell Point across the river from the Holden Seafood Company. He's really harmless. Just gets a bit cranky when he's had too much to drink," Ashley explained as they climbed the stairs.

"Beautiful sunset," Moore commented as he turned at the top of the stairs to look to the west before walking inside.

"Always," Ashley said. They entered and Ashley apologized to the waiting customers for the intrusion, explaining it was no big deal. The two men then returned to their table where a brunette server approached them.

"Hello Ryan," she said as she arrived next to the table.

"Hannah, meet Emerson Moore. He's an old buddy of mine," Ashley started. "Hannah also is my sister," he explained as he turned to Moore.

"Hello Hannah. Is everyone here a family member?" Moore asked smiling.

"No," she grinned. "What can I get you two?"

"I'll start off with a Bud Light," Ashley replied.

"How about you, Emerson?" Hannah asked.

"Sweet tea."

"And do you two know what you'd like for dinner?" Hannah inquired politely.

Both ordered flounder dinners.

When Hannah walked away, Ashley mentioned, "I told you Hannah's engaged to Corbett Holden. He captains the trawler you saw at the dock. Really nice guy. Speaks with a thick North Carolina accent. You'll meet him tomorrow."

"I remember you saying that. I'll look forward to it."

As they waited, Moore looked out to the ocean where the daylight was transforming into night. "There's a boat out there. I saw it when we first came in. It looks like it's just running back and forth," Moore observed.

"Yeah. They've been out there for a few days. Rough crew from what I've heard. Not sure what they're up to."

"It doesn't look like a fishing trawler," Moore commented.

"It isn't. They've come into the marina on the Intracoastal Waterway to fuel up. I hear they're really secretive about what they are up to. They're not fishing or trawling for shrimp, that's for sure."

The two men spent the rest of the evening enjoying their meals and catching up. At closing, Ashley, Rachel and Moore walked over to the docked Sea Hunt and rode back up the Shallotte River. They then walked over to the house to call it a night. Moore grabbed his duffel bag from the car and followed Ashley down the hall to his room. He was tired. It had been a very long day. Within minutes, he was in bed and asleep.

About four hours later, Moore awoke in a cold sweat. He had been dreaming about his last adventure in Louisiana. He rolled over but couldn't fall back asleep. He decided to slip on his jogging shorts and boat shoes to get a breath of fresh air. Moore walked quietly through the house so as not to disturb his sleeping hosts. He carefully eased the front door open and stepped outside where he took in a deep breath of the cool breeze coming upriver from the ocean.

He wandered over to the dock to check out the shrimp trawler and enjoy the river. That's when he noticed a light on the river. He walked down the dock as he tried to allow his eyes to pierce the night. He made out the silhouette of a small boat in the river where he also saw the shadow of a man in the boat. It looked like he was dragging something in the water, but Moore wasn't quite sure. After ten minutes, he returned to the house. He'd find out the next morning when Ryan was awake.

CHAPTER 4

Early the Next Morning
Ashley's House

The rich aroma of bacon cooking greeted Moore's nostrils as he walked into the kitchen.

"That smells so good," Moore commented.

"And tasty. Did you sleep well?" Rachel asked as she turned from the stove.

"I sure did. It was a really long day."

"There's coffee on the counter if you'd like to pour yourself a cup. Ryan is on the porch if you want to join him."

"Thank you." He poured a cup of coffee and joined Ashley on the porch, sitting on one of the wicker chairs.

"All rested up?" Ashley asked.

"Yes. What a view," Moore commented as he looked past the Holden Seafood Company to the river and the marsh grass on the far side.

"This is how I like to start my day. Coffee with this view."

Moore nodded. "Ryan, I have a question for you."

"Fire away, Emerson."

"I woke up in the middle of the night and took a walk down to the dock where your boat is. I saw a light coming from another boat on the river. It looked like its occupant was dragging something in the water. Do you know what that's about?"

"That would be Swaney Swanson. His real first name is Herbert, but he hates it. Don't ever call him Herbert. You don't want to experience his wrath," Ashley warned before continuing. "He's a retired trawler captain. He used to work for the Holdens. That's his house over there. Or maybe I should say shack. I've offered to repair it, but he doesn't want anyone bothering him."

Moore looked to where Ashley was pointing. There was a massive 80-foot-tall North Carolina live oak tree on the riverbank. It had a dark gray, thick trunk that supported large branches spreading out in all directions. Under its leafy canopy of greenery sat a shack with a sagging roof. It looked like it had seen better days.

The paint on the wood siding was peeling off in large flakes to reveal the rotting wood underneath, the roof was partially covered with moss, and the door was hanging by several rusty hinges. A porch with several worn chairs faced the riverbank twenty feet away. The lawn was overgrown with weeds and littered with trash.

There was a small dock that extended fifteen feet into the river. A boat was secured to the dock. It was a light green center console 2019 Bay Rider 2260 with twin 150 HP Yamaha outboard motors. The name *Rainbow's End* was scripted on her stern.

"That place needs some attention," Moore mused.

"I'm waiting for a strong wind to come along and collapse that house," Ashley commented. "It's kind of funny how Swaney is. He doesn't pay any attention to his house, but his boat, its motors and his fishing gear are in immaculate working condition."

Moore turned to Ashley. "Ryan, what was he doing on the river last night?"

"He's kind of secretive about what he is looking for. But rumor has it that he got in an argument with his wife. He grabbed her jewelry box with her wedding band inside and tossed it in the river. After she died, he began this nightly venture. He's searched downriver in case the current carried it away and throughout this area. It may have stuck in the mud and be buried there."

"You think there's something else inside that's real valuable?"

"Not sure. Could be."

"Does he drag the river during the day?"

"No. Just at night. Really strange."

"I'll say," Moore said.

"You boys ready for breakfast?" Rachel called from the kitchen.

The two men grabbed their empty coffee cups and returned inside for their meal.

"Would you look at that! Isn't my wife the best!" Ashley exclaimed as he eyed the egg casserole with cheese and ham.

"That does look good," Moore agreed emphatically.

"Eat up, boys," Rachel smiled.

After they finished eating, Ashley walked Moore next door to meet the owners of Holden Seafood Company. He introduced Moore to the tall, gray-haired Barry and his ravishing blonde wife, Fran.

"You visiting here long?" Fran asked with her deep North Carolina accent as she eyed the handsome visitor.

"Probably ten days of relaxation," Moore answered.

"You came to the right place," Barry suggested. "Staying with Ryan, are you?"

"Yes, unless he kicks me out," Moore grinned.

"I've been known to do that," Ashley quipped.

Two young men entered the retail space of the Holden Seafood Company.

"These are my two sons. This one is Corbett. He captains

that trawler out there," Barry explained as he introduced the tall man with a red beard before pointing to the second one. "This other one is Roddy. He helps out with just about everything around here."

"We always warn the ladies about Roddy," Ashley interjected. "I told you he's a real ladies' man," Ashley teased.

"Hang on a second. I'll show you a sign we had made for the store for when Roddy comes by." Corbett reached behind the counter and produced a sign that he held up for Moore to see. It read "No Shoes! No Shirt! No Roddy!"

Moore chuckled. "You guys like to pick on him?"

"It's all in fun. You ever been on a shrimp trawler, Emerson?" Corbett asked in his North Carolina drawl.

"No, but I'd like to go out with you."

"We can arrange that, but I have to warn you. It's hard work," Corbett cautioned.

"That's not a problem for me," Moore answered.

Corbett nodded his head. "How about tomorrow morning, Emerson?"

"Sounds good to me."

"We'll see you at the dock at 6:00. Can you get up that early?" Corbett jested.

"Sure can. I saw the name on the side of the boat. It read *Capt. C.L. Holden*. Is it named after you?"

"No, Emerson. The trawler is named after my grandfather. He had it built, and it's been passed down through the family. I'm proud to be named after him," Corbett explained.

"We all are," Barry added.

"Folks, I'm burning daylight. I hate to break up this party, but I've got work to do," Ashley said as he moved toward the doorway.

"I'll see you in the morning, Corbett," Moore confirmed. "I'm looking forward to being on that trawler."

They said their goodbyes and left. Once outside, Ashley turned to Moore. "What would you like to do today?"

"I think I'll head over to Holden Beach."

"Good plan. Take my boat. I don't need it, and Rachel needs to pick up supplies in her car for the restaurant. She won't need the boat."

"Thanks. I appreciate it."

"And you can grab lunch at the restaurant if you like."

The two returned to the house. Within a few minutes, Ashley drove away in his Ford F-150 truck, equipped with a serious-looking toolbox and ladder rack.

Moore grabbed his swim trunks, towel and sunscreen. He saw the boat keys on the kitchen counter as he walked through the room. Picking them up, he left the house and walked over to the *My Rachel*. Within minutes he was heading downriver at a slower rate of speed than Ashley the previous night. After turning left onto the Intracoastal Waterway, he spotted the dock that Ashley had used the previous night and pointed the watercraft toward it.

When he finished docking the boat, he walked across the street to Holden Beach and picked out a spot close to the water. Settling on his towel, he soon stretched out in the early morning sun to enjoy the peace and solitude before the island vacationers arrived. Moore must have dozed off as he awoke from the sounds of two boys nearby playing in the sand. He glanced at his watch and saw it was almost noon. Deciding to lunch on the pier, he grabbed his gear and walked toward it.

When he arrived and opened the restaurant door, he was greeted by Chloe. "It's nice to see you again, Emerson," she beamed.

"And you too, Chloe. I didn't realize I'd be back this quick," he smiled at the pretty teenaged blonde.

"Table for one?"

"Yes. By the window if you have one available."

"We sure do."

Moore followed her to a table in the far southeast side. It offered a panoramic view of the ocean and beach below. He quickly reviewed the menu that Chloe provided. It was filled with an array of tempting choices. He settled on sweet tea and a grouper sandwich, then placed his order with his server.

Forty-five minutes later, he had finished his meal and paid the server. Moore sat sipping his tea as he eyed the mysterious boat on the horizon. He thought it was the same one from the previous night. It seemed to be running a pattern, reminding him of the grid shipwreck hunters would run with their boats.

He next saw a 16-foot open bow boat with two occupants. They appeared to have lost power to their motor as they were using oars to paddle toward the beach. They weren't making much progress as the tide was against them.

Seeing their predicament, Moore downed the rest of his tea and left the building. He hurried back to the Sea Hunt and started its motor. Within seconds, he was racing down the Intracoastal Waterway to Shallotte Inlet which led to the ocean. A few minutes later, he rounded the end of Holden Island and headed for the distressed boat. As he neared the boat, he saw that it was occupied by two deeply-tanned, teenage boys who seemed relieved by his approach.

"You boys need a hand?" he asked as he pulled back on the throttle and the Sea Hunt nudged up against their boat.

The brown-haired boy wearing a Holden Seafood Company

t-shirt spoke first. "Sure do." He looked toward the boat on the horizon. "Those dirty…"

The scraggily-haired boy in a worn, torn t-shirt cut him off as he placed his hand on the first boy's arm to caution him. "It's no big thing. Yeah. We need a tow," the blond spoke carefully.

Moore's eyes scanned the boat. He was shocked by what he saw. The boat seemed destined for the salvage yard, not for an open sea adventure. Rather than a runabout boat, it appeared to be a run-away-from boat. The windshield was cracked. There were cracks in the fiberglass hull, and some were covered with duct tape. There was water on the deck, and a couple of bailing cans rolled around next to a hand pump. The seats were worn, and one was broken. It reminded Moore of Swanson's shack.

Moore eyed the rusty, decrepit motor. It had seen its better days, probably in the ice age. "Where's your fuel line?" he asked as he saw the fuel tanks, but no line running from them to the outboard motor.

The first boy's nostrils flared, and his eyes narrowed. He was about to answer when his friend spoke first. "It, ah… it fell overboard," he hemmed and hawed.

Moore wrinkled his brow at the questionable explanation. "You want to try answering my question again?" he asked in a serious tone.

"Like I said. It fell overboard when I was switching tanks."

Moore was skeptical. There was more to their story than what they were willing to share. The two boys looked like the kind who would get in a lot of misadventures together.

"I'm not sure about your craft's seaworthiness. You shouldn't be out here in that leaky hull," Moore remarked in a no-nonsense tone.

"There's nothing wrong with my boat. She's just showing

her character," the second boy explained.

"More like character flaws," Moore stated firmly. "Where can I tow you?" Moore asked, realizing he wouldn't get a straight answer from them.

"Up the Shallotte River. Do you know where the Holden Seafood Company is?" the first boy asked.

"I sure do. I'm staying next door."

The two boys looked at each other for a moment before the first boy continued. "My grandad lives next door. Could you take us to his dock?"

"I can do that. Since we're neighbors, I better introduce myself. I'm Emerson Moore."

The first boy, who seemed be of a responsible nature, replied first. "I'm Holden Swanson."

"Swaney's grandson?" Moore asked.

"Yep."

"Do you live with him?"

"No. Mom and I live up the river about a hundred yards."

"I'm Archie Flynn," Flynn interjected with a sly grin. He looked like he was up to something. He was a mischievous young man with a carefree spirit and disregard for authority. He stepped forward to hand Moore a tow line.

How appropriate, Moore thought. The two young men reminded him of Tom Sawyer and Huck Finn.

"And which of you two fine gentlemen own this fine craft?" Moore asked as he took the line from Flynn.

"This fine shipwreck belongs to me," Flynn replied proudly as Holden started bailing water out of the boat. "I run a charter business," he stated proudly.

"With this boat?" Moore asked in surprise.

"Yessir."

"Been real busy?" Moore asked, thinking he already knew the answer.

"Business has been a bit slow," Flynn replied.

I bet, Moore thought. "And do you live close to Holden?"

"No. I'm up the Shallotte River, almost to Shallotte," Flynn replied.

Moore nodded. "All right then, let's tow you guys upriver."

Thirty minutes later, Moore docked at the Swanson dock on the Shallotte River. As he and the two boys stepped off the boats, a low shout emerged from the sagging porch overlooking the dock.

"Now, what have ya two river rats gone and done?"

They turned their heads toward the porch, and Holden yelled back.

"It's nothing Grandad. Just need a new gas line."

"I told ya boys that it's risky boating around in that hull of shambles. I should call it floating flotsam with a motor I wouldn't put on a lawn mower," Swanson drawled in a voice similar to actor Sam Elliott, slow and deliberate.

Moore chuckled softly at the spot-on description as he watched the slightly-built, seventy-year-old pop up from a rusty metal chair and amble toward them.

Below Swanson's calm outward appearance was a hidden reserve of energy, ready to burst out when necessary. His high energy level would match any forty-year-old. People were amazed by his ability and work ethic. He probably could outwork half the county.

He wore a blue Carolina Panthers ballcap with uncombed graying hair sticking out. The cap color matched the twinkling blue in his eyes. His face had a thick, brushy mustache that hung halfway over his lips. There were heavy wrinkles on his forehead from his time in the sun on the fishing trawlers. He would tell people that the wrinkles and his gnarled hands were the signs of a hard-working man.

Swanson kept pretty much to himself, not sticking his nose in everybody's business. People would still find their way down to his shack under the huge live oak on the riverbank. They'd go to him for advice because the old man had seen a lot and kept his mouth shut. He didn't carry on and tell everyone what he had heard or knew. People liked that about him. He was known for keeping a confidence.

The retiree would help anyone in need without expecting anything in return. Although everyone knew that he had a fondness for homemade blueberry pies. Every once in a while, he'd find one dropped off on his rickety porch on top of that old table with the blue and white checkered plastic tablecloth.

Every morning, Swanson would slip into a worn t-shirt and jeans. He'd start out the day with a cup of hot coffee on the porch overlooking the river. The steam arising from the coffee cup matched the early morning mist coming off the river. When he finished, he'd go inside and make himself some cinnamon toast. He'd slather it with butter and strawberry jam, then devour it while fixing himself another cup of coffee.

Once he was done, he'd amble down to the shed and the dock to check on his boat. Once he knew it was still secure, he might head inside the shed to tinker a bit or load up the boat and head downriver to the inlet and out into the Atlantic to fish. Swanson loved fishing. Every once in a while, he'd get a call to help out on one of the trawlers when they were a man short for the day. He loved getting the calls. Swanson wouldn't use a smartphone. He still had the flip phone he got years ago.

"Grandad, this is Emerson Moore. He kind of helped us

out today. He's staying with Ryan and Rachel Ashley," Holden volunteered as Swanson approached.

"I'm Swanson. Folks around here call me Swaney," Swanson said as he extended his right hand to Moore.

Moore shook it as he saw that Swanson was missing two fingers. When Swanson noticed Moore's glance, as little escaped his sharp eyes, he commented, "Gator took my fingers if yar wondering."

"You should have seen Grandad. I was here that day," Holden beamed proudly. "That gator creeped up on the bank right here and tried to snatch Grandad's Yorkie. It had little Shrimphead in his mouth when Grandad ran over to it and pried Shrimphead out of the gator's mouth. But the gator snapped down and tore off two of Grandad's fingers."

"Yep, and I've been waiting for that gator to reappear." Swanson pointed to the nearby porch where a shotgun leaned against the wall. "I'm ready for him."

"Is that Shrimphead on the porch?" Moore asked as he saw a small Yorkie laying on its belly.

"That would be Shrimphead. He knows to stay away from the river's edge."

Moore looked to the river. "Does that alligator come around here often?"

"I call him Leatherhead. He's about 15-foot long and lives upriver. He only comes down with the fresh water when the tide runs out. He goes back upriver when the tide comes in and brings saltwater into the river. Them gators don't have saltwater glands like their crocodile brethren," Swanson explained before adding, "I'll get him one day." He nodded his head affirmatively.

Moore saw a stuffed toy dog by the dock. "Is that your bait?"

"Well, aren't you the educated man!" Swanson sneered in his slow drawl before turning his attention to the boys. "It sure is," he exclaimed.

"I wish you well in catching him," Moore offered, ignoring the sneering remark.

"What happened with the boat? Looks like yar missing a fuel line," Swanson questioned as he eyed the watercraft.

Immediately the boys' countenance shifted. They began hemming and hawing.

"I get it. Ya don't want to tell me," Swanson commented. "But ya will," he added in a solemn tone.

"This looks like a serious discussion," an approaching feminine voice called.

The group turned to see a striking blonde in her late thirties walking toward them.

"It nothing, Mom," Holden answered quickly, but nervously. He didn't want her probing into what really happened to the two boys. "We were just talking to our new neighbor. He's staying with Ryan and Rachel," Holden gushed.

"Oh you are, are you?" she asked with disbelief as she turned to eye Moore. She could always tell when her son was up to no good, especially when he was with the Flynn boy. "I'm Dottie Swanson," she smiled.

"Emerson Moore," Moore replied, awestruck by her beauty.

"You visiting here for long?" she asked.

"Probably ten days or so."

"I hope you enjoy your stay." She turned to Swanson. "Dad, could you give me a ride over to the restaurant? My car is in the shop."

Moore's eyes swung to the old yellow pickup truck with dents on the side of the bed and the front grill. It was parked next to Swanson's house. "Swaney, it looks like your right front tire is low," he observed.

"That's not a problem. Holden, get down there and put yar mouth on that valve stem. Ya can blow it up for me," Swanson joked.

Flynn interjected himself into the conversation. "You haven't ridden with anyone until you've had a ride with Swaney. He terrorizes people with the way he drives. The police show up real regular like to give him a talking to," he chuckled.

Swanson shot the boy a sharp glance and the smile disappeared from Flynn's face.

"He's not that bad," Dottie commented as she shook her head. "Fess up, Archie."

"I was just joshing," he replied as he peered up from under his bowed head at Swanson.

"I can give you a lift. My car is right over there," Moore said as he pointed at his Mustang convertible parked by the Ashley house.

"Can we come?" Holden asked when he saw the car.

"No." Swanson answered before Moore could respond. "Ya boys still have some explaining to do and that's what we're going to focus on."

The boys looked crestfallen.

"Another time. I'll give you boys a ride," Moore said, turning to Dottie. "Where do you need to go?"

"The Flounder Pier restaurant. I'm a server there."

Moore looked back at Ashley's boat. "I can just take you back in the boat. That would be faster," he offered.

"Sure. That works," she smiled as she followed him to the watercraft. "You boys listen to Grandad, understand?" she called.

Both boys nodded as she stepped aboard the Sea Hunt. Within a minute, it was moving downriver.

"Holden seems like a fine young man," Moore said as he opened the conversation.

"I'm very proud of him. He's a good boy. He's got a lot of the traits of his grandad. People seem to gravitate to him like Archie."

"Now that one looks a bit ornery to me," Moore commented. "Is his real name Archie?"

"No. It's Harold, but people started calling him Archie. I don't know why," she smiled. "He has a touch of orneriness, but he's a good boy at heart."

"That boy needs a better boat. I wouldn't go out on it," Moore commented. "I wouldn't be surprised that it has major structural damage the way its leaking."

Dottie laughed. "Did they show you how the boat pump works?"

"No."

"Archie stands in the stern and holds two wires together to get the pump to work. I keep telling them to get it fixed, but he doesn't want to bother anyone."

"I bet Swaney could fix it in a jiff. I heard he's pretty handy with boats."

"He could, but no, Archie won't ask him."

"Does Flynn live nearby?" Moore asked, forgetting that Flynn had told him earlier.

"Upriver. Closer to Shallotte. Poor boy doesn't have a father. Mother is an alcoholic and doesn't pay him any attention. Nor does she care about him."

"That's sad."

Dottie nodded. "I'm glad that Holden is trying to have a

positive influence on him. At times, I wonder if it's Archie having a negative influence on Holden. They seem to always be getting in trouble together."

"Serious?"

"Not really. Just teenage boys being teenage boys. Doing some of the dumb stuff that we all did at that age." She paused for a moment before asking, "By the way, where did you find the boys?"

"They were offshore."

"In the Atlantic?" she asked with concern in her voice.

"Yes."

"I'm going to have to talk with Holden tonight. I told him that he wasn't allowed to go out in the Atlantic in that boat. There's too much of a chance that something serious could happen."

"I agree."

"Sometimes I have to reel him in. Especially with his father being gone," she said frustrated.

"Is he away for work?" Moore asked.

"Hank passed away shortly after our divorce two years ago. He was working a trawler and fell overboard. His body was never recovered," she responded as if she was talking about the weather.

It was obvious to Moore that there was no love lost for her former husband.

"I'm sorry," Moore offered sympathetically.

"He was a tough man to be around. But enough talk about that. What kind of work do you do?"

"I'm an investigative reporter."

"That sounds interesting," she responded as Moore turned left into the Intracoastal Waterway. He pulled back on the throttle slightly to slow the Sea Hunt as he was enjoying the conversation.

"Do you work in Raleigh?" she asked.

"Actually, I work out of my aunt's house on South Bass Island in the western basin of Lake Erie – in Ohio. Ever been to Lake Erie?"

"No."

"It's beautiful up there. It's like Holden Beach, but with more entertainment, restaurants and places to visit," Moore explained.

"Nothing like having an island in your life," she said as he nudged the watercraft up to the dock.

Shutting off the engine, he volunteered, "I'll walk you over to the restaurant."

"What a gentleman! I'm not used to that," she smiled.

When they reached the door to the restaurant, Dottie turned to Moore. "Have you met the pretty hostess, Chloe?"

"I did. I understand she's Ryan's sister."

"That's not all she is," Dottie said with a sly grin.

"Oh?"

"Holden is a bit sweet on her."

A smile crossed Moore's face. "Teenage love."

"That's right. It's kind of fun watching the two of them. He's a bit awkward around her. Doesn't know what to do."

"I think I'll enjoy this."

Opening the door, Dottie commented, "Thanks for walking me over. I hope you enjoy the rest of your day."

"I plan on it," Moore said as the door closed behind her. He retraced his steps to the beach where he relaxed for another hour before boating back to the dock at the Holden Seafood Company. After docking the Sea Hunt, Moore walked over to the Ashley house and took a brief shower. Since Ashley had texted him that he was tied up on a project, Moore decided to drive up to Shallotte to grab dinner in town.

It was a short drive to Wing and Fish Company on Main Street where Moore ordered a flounder dinner. He just couldn't get enough fresh flounder. When he returned to the Ashley house, he saw Ryan relaxing on the porch.

"How did your day go?" Ashley asked as Moore plopped into a nearby chair. "Relaxing?"

"In some ways. Interesting in others."

"Oh?"

Upon hearing Moore's summary of the day's events, Ashley commented, "You've met more of our neighbors."

"I did, and those boys should never have been out in that ocean in that boat. They're lucky to have made it back," a perturbed Moore answered.

Ashley nodded. "How did you like Swaney?"

"That guy is a character. I'd love to spend some time with him. I bet he has some tales to spin."

Smiling as he shook his head affirmatively, Ashley commented, "And then some. Do you remember Neville from last night - the guy we had to escort out of the Flounder Pier?"

"Yes."

Ashley pointed across the river to the far side. It was about 1,500 feet away. "That's Shell Point over there. If you see a house with red lights on the porch, that's Neville's place."

"Why the red lights?"

"He calls them warning lights. Danger. Watch out!"

"What?" Moore asked, not understanding.

"He likes to keep people at arm's length. Plus, the flashing lights can be seen easily from Swaney's front porch. Neville likes to irritate Swaney and remind Swaney that he's nearby."

"What's that all about?"

"Years ago, Neville and Swaney were best buds. They worked the trawlers together and competed as captains to see who had the best crew and could bring in the best haul of shrimp. It started as a friendly rivalry, but it took a bad turn."

"What happened?"

"Swaney's wife was part of Swaney's crew. They were out several miles when she came down with a ruptured appendix. Her belly was full of infection. They called it peritonitis. She had been complaining about pain in her abdomen, but it was the busy season and she wanted to tough it out. She passed out on the deck and Swaney headed the trawler for Wilmington to get her to the hospital. Then, his engine failed. He radioed Neville for help since he saw his trawler on the horizon. Neville never came to his aid. By the time the Coast Guard got there, she had died. They said later at the hospital that she had sepsis in her bloodstream."

"And Neville ignored Swaney's radio calls for help?" Moore asked in disbelief.

"Neville brought his trawler in with a record catch of shrimp. When Swaney returned and confronted him, Neville tried to explain that his radio wasn't working. His crew said the same thing, but Swaney didn't believe him. He even went aboard and tried the radio. It worked. He wouldn't believe Neville when he said he had a guy repair it as soon as they docked."

"That is so sad," Moore commented as he shook his head from side to side.

"Later, Neville would find his nets sabotaged. He blamed Swaney. They got into a pretty big fistfight on the dock. It took six guys to pull them apart. The sheriff had a heart-to-heart with both of them. He told them to cut it out or they'd be answering to him."

"So they don't talk to each other at all?" Moore asked.

"Not one peep. They do their best to ignore each other, but they still like to jab at each other when they have a chance. Like the flashing red light, but no more physical scuffles."

"Too bad that they can't work things out."

"Those two have more twists in their relationship than there were in Chubby Checker's dance moves," Ashley cracked.

Chuckling, Moore took one last look at the flashing red lights across the river before turning to Ashley. "I guess I'd better turn in. I'm on the trawler in the morning."

"You'll get worn out, but I'm sure that you'll love every minute of it."

CHAPTER 5

Early Next Morning
Holden Seafood Company Dock

The morning sky was a soft blend of purple and pink as it transcended into first light with the rosy fingers of the sun's rays stretching across the horizon. The air was cool and fresh as Moore approached the dock where the trawler was gently rocking.

The all-white trawler was 80-feet long with a 22-foot beam. She was powered by a CAT 1150 375HP diesel engine. Her outriggers were upright like two sentinels on dawn watch. Her name was written across the stern and on the bow. It read *Capt. C.L. Holden*.

Moore saw Corbett standing outside the wheelhouse.

"Come on Emerson. We're burning daylight," he shouted, anxious to put to sea.

"It's not daylight yet," Moore countered.

"It is on my shrimp boat clock. Now get yourself aboard," he called. "Lacey has coffee ready for you."

Moore scurried aboard as Quint and Roddy released the lines, and Corbett returned inside the wheelhouse. Within seconds, the boat was headed downriver with the outgoing tide.

"Morning Quint," Moore greeted the young, blond crewman.

"Morning. It's a good day for shrimping, Emerson. There's coffee in the galley." Quint pointed to an open door on the port side of the boat.

"I could use a cup," Moore responded as he went into the galley.

"Lacey makes good coffee," Roddy added.

"Nothing like a good cup of coffee to start the day," Moore agreed.

When Moore entered the small galley, he found the other member of the crew, Lacey. He had a cup of hot coffee ready for him. "Cream and sugar are over there," he pointed. "Help yourself. I'm not the designated coffee server," he teased.

"Black is fine," Moore said as he sipped the hot brew. He went down a passageway and up several steps into the wheelhouse to join Corbett, who was seated with one hand on the helm.

"Ready for your first shrimping experience, are ya?"

"I am," Moore said as he saw a sign on the wheelhouse wall. It read "Fishing stories told here…some true." He laughed softly.

"I hope it's a good one. My family has been shrimping here for generations. We know every nook and cranny in these seas," Corbett drawled.

The two chatted casually over the next fifteen minutes as Moore asked questions about shrimping.

"Looks like we may have fair seas today," Corbett affirmed as the boat crossed the Intracoastal Waterway and passed through the inlet to the Atlantic Ocean.

"That's good. How far are we going out?"

"Just out to the horizon. You'll be able to see the Flounder Pier from where we'll be working." Corbett turned his head to Moore. "Ryan told you that we'd be out here from today through Thursday, right?"

"Yes. And he's going to pick me up late this afternoon." Moore didn't want to be on the trawler from Sunday through Thursday, working like Corbett and the crew. He only wanted a taste of what it was like.

"We'll return on high tide Thursday so the fresh shrimp will be ready for the weekend sales," Corbett explained.

A few minutes passed before Corbett continued. "You need to come out with us when we have some rough seas. I've been out here in 20-foot seas. I've seen trawlers disappear between the swells, but that's the life we lead."

Moore's eyes widened. "Not sure I'd enjoy that."

"We don't either, but that's a part of the shrimping business."

"I like the feel of solid land under my feet," Moore countered.

"I've been in seas so bad that I wished I had on a diaper under my pants," Corbett joked.

"That bad!"

Corbett nodded. "I've been in waves as tall as a two-story building. Makes your knees turn to jelly and the check engine light on your heart flash like a strobe light."

Moore snickered softly at the humorous explanation as they continued their conversation.

Thirty minutes later, Corbett commented, "You might want to go join the crew. They'll be lowering the outriggers."

Moore nodded as he left the wheelhouse and went midship where he saw Lacey, Roddy and Quint lowering the outriggers. "What are those outriggers for?" he asked Lacey.

"They help stabilize the boat, but their main purpose is to keep each side of the nets separate so they don't get tangled up."

After they lowered the stabilizers, they began to use the block and tackle to lower two wooden doors which were attached to the leg lines of the net.

"What's that about?" Moore asked as he watched with keen

interest.

"Those doors help keep the nets open," Roddy explained.

Once the doors were lowered, Lacey suggested, "Emerson, you can help us unfold the nets."

Moore began assisting them. "How do these nets work?"

"They're kind of a bottom trawl. One end is weighted, and it's pulled behind the boat as it skims the bottom. It's like a flattened cone. The top end of the net has floats on it to keep it up and open. The back end of the net is called the bag. It's where the catch collect. Shrimp go into the front end of the net and are funneled to the back. We catch them one drag at a time as Corbett drops the trawler speed to 2.5 knots."

Moore noticed Quint tying lines around the end of the bags. "What are you doing there, Quint?"

"We tie these lines in a special way that can hold the weight of the catch, but can be easily untied with a quick pull. You'll see when we pull the nets," he smiled.

When the four nets were ready, the men eased them overboard, two on each side.

"What was that chain I saw?" Moore asked when they finished.

"That's what we call a tickler. That chain skims the bottom in front of the net. It makes the shrimp jump so that they are swept into the approaching net," Lacey said.

"The net has a turtle escape device so that any sea turtles that might get caught accidently can swim out," Roddy added.

"That's not the only escape device in the net. There's a by-catch reduction device which allows fish to swim out through a flap if they get caught in the net," Lacey explained.

"I guess you wouldn't want to haul sharks aboard," Moore responded with a smile.

"You might get some small ones. There's always some small fish caught up too. You'll see," Lacey replied.

"And those blacktip thresher sharks are real aggressive when they get caught. They can destroy a net," Quint added.

Two hours later, the crew used the winch in the center of the boat to haul aboard the nets. The bag ends were swung over the open area behind the winches and the bag lines were popped, dumping the large catch of grayish-white shrimp on the deck.

"Grab yourself one of those plastic milk cartons and a rake. It's culling time," Lacey directed.

Moore did as instructed and took a position near Lacey who had rigged an awning over the deck where the shrimp had been piled.

"We need to cull the catch. That means we need to sort out any fish or damaged and dead shrimp first. You just rake out the bad catch and shove it through the scuppers," Lacey explained.

Moore looked behind him to the openings in the gunwales that also allowed water from high waves to drain off the deck. "Got it," he answered as he joined the three men in culling.

"It's seagull feeding time. That's why we got all of those noisy seagulls following us," Quint mentioned.

Moore looked behind the trawler stern and saw the hungry scavengers waiting for their meal as they swooped and squawked, their noise piercing the ocean air above the low hum of the trawler diesel engines. After they finished culling the catch, they headed the shrimp as they sorted them by size into baskets. They next placed the baskets below deck and covered them with layers of ice from the ice bins.

As the process was repeated throughout the day, Moore was eagerly looking forward to Ashley's arrival to take him back to the dock. It had been a long day with a brief lunch break for cold baloney sandwiches and bottles of water.

Late afternoon brought the sounds of an approaching boat. Roddy stood and recognized the watercraft. "Emerson, your taxi is here."

While Roddy helped secure Ashley's boat to the trawler, Moore thanked the crew and headed to the wheelhouse to thank Corbett for the experience. When he returned, the crew had finished loading several containers of freshly-caught shrimp into Ashley's boat for the Flounder Pier.

"Nothing like fresh shrimp for my restaurant customers," Ashley said as Moore stepped aboard the Sea Hunt. "How did your day go?"

Moore groaned as he sat next to Ashley at the center console. "I'm beat, but I have a new appreciation for the hard work that takes place on a shrimp boat. You really have to love what you do," Moore commented.

"Not like that desk job you have as an investigative reporter," Ashley joked, although he knew from past conversations that Moore had been in some rough situations during his field work.

Moore smiled. "I'll keep my day job. It sure is easier than what they go through and in all kinds of weather. I wouldn't want to be out here in high seas."

"Me neither," Ashley agreed as he opened the throttle and pointed the watercraft toward Holden Beach.

They hadn't gone far before Moore saw the mysterious 30-foot Island Hopper with its forward cabin running its grid. "Ryan, do you think we could head over there to see what they're doing?"

"Sure," Ashley replied as he changed their course.

A few minutes later, they approached and saw the name

Aft Kicker displayed on her stern. Two rough-looking men were standing near the stern with frowns on their face as they watched the approaching boat. Another was at the helm.

"Ahoy!" Ashley called as he cut back on the throttle.

"Back off," the bearded, stern-faced man with a scarred eye shouted. His name was Derek Binder. He didn't like people snooping around him when he was working.

"In a sec. We just wondered what you all were up to," Ashley yelled. "I see you guys from the Flounder Pier and wondered what you were looking for. Just curious if you don't mind."

"I do mind. Now back off," Binder called back as he bent below the gunwale and reappeared with a shotgun in his hands.

"No need for that. Sorry. Didn't mean to intrude," Ashley apologized as he wheeled the Sea Hunt to port and smartly moved the throttle forward.

Binder briefly watched them before returning the shotgun to the deck.

"What was that about?" Moore asked incredulously as the Sea Hunt extended its departure.

"Someone who is very private or someone who doesn't want anyone to know what they are doing."

"My sixth sense tells me that they are up to no good," Moore offered.

"What an appropriate name for that boat! *Aft Kicker*! If I wasn't in such a hurry to get in this load of shrimp, I may have taken a little time to do some aft kicking myself.

Moore laughed.

"That jack aft can just kiss my aft. Let's bust aft and get the aft out of here." Ashley was on a roll as he opened the throttle.

"Ryan, you crack me up," Moore grinned.

"Oh, that's nothing. I told Rachel that my next boat would

be named *Sweaty Test Tackles*."

"Ryan, you're incorrigible."

Their banter continued under the Holden Beach bridge and to the dock where they unloaded the baskets of fresh shrimp into Ashley's parked truck.

"If you don't mind Emerson, could you run the Sea Hunt back up to the Holden Seafood Company?"

"I sure can," Moore replied.

"I'm going to be helping out at the restaurant. There's food in the fridge at the house if you don't mind fixing your own dinner."

"Ryan, I'd welcome a quiet evening. I'm bushed from shrimping all day. I've used muscles that I haven't used in years."

Laughing, Ashley remarked, "I bet you're sore. Just be glad that you're not out there for four days at a time."

"That I am," Moore said as he stepped back aboard the Sea Hunt.

While Ashley drove over to the restaurant, Moore steered the Sea Hunt down the Intracoastal Waterway to the Shallotte River. After docking her upriver at the Holden Seafood Company, he walked over to the Ashley house. He headed to his room, then took a quick shower to allow the warm water to soothe his aching body. After slipping on a shirt and shorts, he walked into the kitchen where he made a salad and ham sandwich. Moore took them out to the porch where he gobbled them down as he watched the approaching night cast its darkness on the Shallotte River.

Sipping his sweet tea, he speed-dialed his old buddy Ralph "Willie" Wilbanks who lived about four hours away on the other side of Charleston, South Carolina. He had some questions for his underwater archaeologist friend with whom he had shared several high-action adventures in Key West.

Wilbanks had an M.A. in maritime history and underwater archaeology from East Carolina University's Maritime Studies Program. He specialized in maritime history of the Great Lakes, the Florida Keys and World War II. He was also internationally known for his role in the discovery of the *H.L. Hunley* in 1995. The Confederate combat submarine sank during the Civil War on February 17,1864 following its sinking of the Union warship USS *Housatonic* during military engagement in Charleston Harbor.

"Emerson, it's about time y'all gave us a call," a sweet, feminine voice answered.

Moore recognized Mrs. Wilbanks' voice right away. "Hello Anne," Moore replied to the slender, brunette who wore rimless glasses.

"When are y'all going to get your butt down here for a visit?" she asked with an accent that matched Wilbanks' southern accent.

"It's been a while," Moore thought as he recalled his last visit to their island home. He loved spending time at their house, which was like a nautical museum, filled with deep diving helmets, small cannons, and other underwater findings. Moore once had spent the night in their small guest house that Wilbanks had named the Snore House.

"Too long. Y'all get yourself down here real quick, now," she insisted. "Here's Ralph." She handed the phone to Wilbanks.

"Do I hear y'all givin' my wife a hard time?" the 68-year-old, gray-haired and mustached Southern charmer greeted Moore.

"He never answered my question!" Anne shouted in the background.

"Okay. I'll ask him again. When are y'all going to get your butt down here?"

"I'll see what I can do."

"There ya'll go. Pissing on my leg and telling me it's raining. That's no answer, boy," Wilbanks pushed.

"I don't know. I'm in Shallotte…"

Wilbanks cut him off. "Gawd boy. Shallotte is only fours hours away. Y'all get yourself down here."

"He's in Shallotte?" Anne asked in the background.

"Emerson's brain is rattling around like a BB in a box car. Y'all are that close and not stopping in. I've got a tree stump in my backyard with a higher IQ than y'all, Emerson." Wilbanks was on a roll.

"Give him a chance to answer, Ralph," Anne remarked.

Moore was grinning. He loved to hear the wise-cracking southerner prattle on. "I will try to make it down after I finish with my visit here."

"Ya'll working?"

"Not really."

"Y'all are," Wilbanks quickly deducted. He knew Moore's penchant for getting involved in things when he should be off the clock. "What are y'all up to?"

"I've been spending some time on Holden Beach."

"I know the area. I've spent some time shipwreck hunting there."

"Can you tell me about the area?" Moore asked as he settled back to hear this legend share his vast knowledge of East Coast shipwrecks.

"I can, Emerson. There are primarily four Civil War shipwrecks in the area. If y'all go to the east end of Holden Island, y'all see Lockwood Folley Inlet between Oak Island and Holden

Island," Wilbanks began in a serious tone.

"The blockade runner CSS *Elizabeth* was the first of the four to sink. She was returning with a cargo of steel and saltpeter from Nassau on a run to Wilmington on the Cape Fear River. She ran aground, and the captain set her on fire to avoid capture.

"Next to her is the iron-hulled paddle-wheeler CSS *Bendigo*. She was returning from Nassau to Wilmington. She ran hard aground when her captain thought he saw a Union ship approaching. They were able to offload her cargo before the captain set her afire and abandoned the ship. Her wreck is marked by an orange navigation warning buoy because she's a hazard for local watercraft as are the other three. Y'all can see the base of her funnel and part of the superstructure during low tide.

"The Union sent the *Montgomery* and *Iron Age* to pull the *Bendigo* from the sand, but they ended up going aground. The *Montgomery* was pulled free, but the *Iron Age* remained aground and had to be sunk.

"Then y'all have the sinking of the Confederate blockade runner *Ranger*. She was an iron-hulled, sidewheel steamer, heading to Wilmington from Murrells Inlet. She ran aground when she spotted Union ships approaching her.

"These 200-feet long shipwrecks are in shallow water. They are navigational hazards to passing watercraft. Just a real mess, damaging unsuspecting boaters who run into them," Wilbanks said in summary.

"Sure is a shipwreck graveyard," Moore noted.

"Did y'all realize that Holden Island has streets named Rangers Street, Elizabeth Street and Bendigo Street? They're all named after the shipwrecks," Wilbanks explained.

"No. I haven't had a chance to check out the island much. My transit to the island has been by boat and limited to the Flounder Pier and beach below."

"They've got good food there." Wilbanks paused, then asked, "Why are y'all so interested in shipwrecks off Holden Island?"

"There's a bunch of shady characters here on an Island Hopper. It looks to me like they are running a grid straight out from the Flounder Pier. They are very secretive from what I've been told and observed firsthand. Do you know of any shipwrecks in that area?"

"No. The ones I've worked on have been east of Holden Island in Lockwood Folly Inlet. But y'all let me do some checking. Y'all got my mind going, Emerson."

"I'd appreciate that."

"Maybe I'll head up to the archives at South Carolina's Department of Archives and History in Columbia. They've got over 325 years of South Carolina history, including nautical paperwork. Maybe I can dig up something, and if I do, it comes with a cost," Wilbanks suggested in a conspiratorial tone.

"What's it going to cost me?"

"Y'all bring that cotton pickin' butt of yours down here for a visit. Deal?"

"Deal," Moore agreed. "I really do appreciate it, Ralph."

The two ended the call and Moore spent another half hour on the porch before calling it a night. He felt some pain in his ribs and hoped he didn't cause a setback in their healing. He may have overdone it that day.

As he dropped on his bed, he made a mental note to get up in the middle of the night to see if Swanson was on the river again. He quickly fell into a deep sleep. His mental note evaporated the moment he closed his eyes, and he missed checking for Swanson.

CHAPTER 6

**The Next Morning
Ashley's House**

"What do you have planned for today, Emerson?" Ashley asked as the two men ate a breakfast of pancakes and bacon.

"I thought I'd drive down to Islands Art & Books in Ocean Isle Beach. I want to check out some artwork they have. There's a painting of shrimp trawlers that I might buy to take home with me."

"Ocean Isle Beach is only 20 minutes away," Ashley added.

"Good. I'll check them out, then maybe head over to Holden Beach to catch some rays."

"You can take the Sea Hunt if you like."

"Thanks, but I'm going to drive there. I haven't had a good chance to check out the island."

"Sure. I understand. If you change your mind, the keys are on the counter," Ashley pointed.

"Thanks."

The men chatted for a few more minutes as they finished their meal. When Moore left the house, he lowered the Mustang convertible top to enjoy the fresh morning air and partly cloudy sky. As he pulled out of the driveway, he glanced at Swanson's place. He saw the Flynn boy's boat was still docked there.

Twenty minutes later, he pulled off Beach Drive and parked in the Islands Art & Books parking lot. The quaint, white one-story building had large floor-to-ceiling windows that enticed passersby to enter. Opening the door, Moore entered the inviting gallery, filled with coastal artwork, local books and jewelry. He was overcome by a sense of the islands as he looked around.

"Can I help you?" a sun-tanned, white-haired man asked as he walked from the rear of the store. He was jovial with a congenial personality. There was a certain magnetism about him that made people very comfortable and welcome.

"You sure can. I'm Emerson Moore. I just got to the area a few days ago. I'm interested in the paintings of Ivey Hayes."

"I am so glad that you stopped in. I'm Gary Pope," Pope said graciously with a touch of southern charm. "This is my gallery and Ivey's work is right over here."

He led Moore to a corner where the paintings and prints were displayed.

"I just love the colors," Moore said as his eyes took in the artwork with its vivid colors.

"Yes, Ivey had an eye for incredibly bright colors that only he could blend together with his special magic. They kind of jump off the canvass at you, don't you think?"

"Yes. I had planned on buying a print of the Holden Beach painting, the one with the shrimp trawlers. But seeing all of these in person really makes it tough. They are so incredible. I like this beach chair print and the blue heron print," Moore mentioned in awe. "Does Ivey live around here?"

"No. He passed away in 2012, but he left a legacy of his love for the North Carolina coastline. He is among our most popular and beloved contemporary artists – a true legend."

"I'll take the trawler print," Moore decided. "The trawlers are special to me."

"Wonderful. I'll wrap it for you."

"Take your time. I'm going to wander through your gallery," Moore said as he began taking in the rich array of coastal paintings/prints, jewelry and books on display.

Fifteen minutes later, Moore walked over to the counter to pay for his purchase.

"Where are you staying?" Pope asked as he handled the transaction.

"Over by the Holden Seafood Company."

"Are you staying with Fran and Barry?" Pope inquired.

"No. Their neighbor, Ryan Ashley."

"Don't think I know Ryan, but I do know Fran and Barry. They're good people."

"Yes, they are," Moore agreed. "Were you raised here?" Moore asked intrigued by the man's friendly nature.

"No. Greater New York area. Moved down here to help my dad when he owned a resort on Holden Beach. After he sold it, I started this gallery and now run a marketing business for the island communities. Plus, I play guitar in several bands," Pope said as he handed the print to Moore.

Moore was so engrossed in conversing with the gregarious man that he found it difficult to leave.

"Gary, it has been an absolute delight to meet you and talk with you. Your energy level is inspiring," Moore commented as he reluctantly turned for the door.

"Stop back in when you have a chance. Maybe I'll talk you into another of Ivey's prints," Pope smiled as Moore left.

Moore placed the print carefully in the trunk of the Mustang and paused to take in the ambiance of the gallery before driving back to Shallotte. He'd love to visit the gallery one more time if things worked out.

CHAPTER 7

Later That Morning
Shallotte Point

As Moore drove down Bill Holden Road, he spotted Swanson on his porch. He drove over and parked next to Swanson's pickup truck.

Walking over to Swanson, he called, "Good morning Swaney."

Swanson's head slowly but deliberately turned to the side to see who was approaching. Recognizing Moore, he returned the greeting. "Morning, although it's nearly noon."

"I guess that would be right," Moore said as he leaned against the porch rail. He looked at Flynn's boat, commenting, "She's still afloat."

"Not for long if he doesn't get some work done on that semi-floating piece of wreckage. I told the Flynn boy that I'd help him pull her out and work on it. I'm not going to fix it for him, although it wouldn't take me long to fix the hull. I'd rather the boy learnt how to do it. That way he can fix it in the future," he muttered slowly.

"Is Flynn around?"

"No. I gave him a ride home yesterday. He was supposed to come back down here today. I haven't seen hide nor hair of him yet."

"Did the boys ever explain what really happened to the gas line yesterday?" Moore asked curiously.

"Getting the truth out of them was more work than a cat covering crap on a marble floor."

"So they didn't tell you," Moore guessed.

"I didn't say that. Ya see there's one thing about me. I'm relentless. I told them two doodlebugs I'd take them out to the woodshed, and they better have given their hearts to Jesus because their butts were going to be mine. Holden knew right away as to what I was getting at. He's been switched enough times by me when he was younger," Swanson explained with a wry smile.

"What did they tell you?" Moore probed.

"Not what I wanted to hear!" Swanson grumbled as his face turned red with anger. "Them boys was out in the Atlantic in that tub full of holes. First, they had no business being out there in a craft that wasn't seaworthy. Bad things happen out there. Been there. Done that."

Moore watched as the red-hot magma of anger began to rise in the once dormant human volcano.

"Second," he continued, "they ignored a busy boater's orders to back off. They went and nudged right up against some guy's boat and found a shotgun stuck in their faces, while another guy jumps in their boat and pulls off the gas line before throwing it in the water."

"Oh no." Moore eyes popped at hearing the tale.

"They're just lucky that ya came along and saved their butts," he stormed before cooling down a bit. "I should say thank ya for rescuing my grandson and the Flynn boy."

"No problem. Glad to have been able to help. Did anyone report this to the Coast Guard?"

"Nah. That's a waste of time. No witnesses. Adults in a fancy boat against some local mischievous kids. Who do ya think they will listen to?" Swanson cocked his head as he looked directly in Moore's eyes.

"I guess you're right."

"Damn straight, I am," Swanson stated firmly. "I'll keep an eye out for that boat. There are a lot of ways to pay back those type of people. It's called the *Aft Kicker* if ya ever see her."

Moore decided not to relate his run-in with that boat. Instead, he asked, "Swaney, I'd like to ask you a question if you don't mind?"

"Ask away. If I mind, I'll be the first to tell ya."

"A couple of nights ago, I saw you out in the river. It looked like you were looking for something. What was it?"

"I mind," he commented stoically.

"You mind me asking the question?" Moore asked.

Swanson cocked his head at Moore and stared at him with his steely blue eyes. "I mind ya asking and I'm not answering yar question. My biz."

The way he responded, Moore knew that the topic was off limits. He decided to give it some time and bring it up at a later date.

"Hey Grandad," Holden called as he rounded the corner of the house.

"Sleeping to noon?" Swanson asked.

Holden grinned. "Nope. Mom had some chores for me before she went to work. I just finished. Is Archie here?"

"I haven't seen him since yesterday."

"He was going to meet me here so we could fix his boat," Holden stated.

"Haven't seen him." Swanson stood. "I've got to drain the monster," he said as he walked inside.

"That means he's taking a piss," Holden explained to Moore. "Listen. Nobody takes a piss like my Grandad."

Moore's brow wrinkled. He didn't understand what Holden was getting at.

Suddenly, Swanson's deep baritone voice could be heard as he sung. *"Way down upon de Swaney Ribber. Far, far away. Dere's wha my heart is turnin' ebber, dere's wha de old folks stay."*

"Grandad loves singing about the Swaney Ribber," Holden mocked with a large smile.

Swanson repeated the verse another time before he finished. They heard the toilet flush and the water run into his bathroom sink before he returned to join them.

"That's better," Swanson said as he eased himself in a chair and reached down to pet his Yorkie.

"I should be going. I'm going to drive over to Holden Beach," Moore decided.

"Could I ride along?" Holden asked as he eyed the bright red convertible. "I could be your guide and you promised I could take a ride in it."

"Sure. Why not?" Moore replied, thinking he might get some more information about the boy's grandfather's nightly searches.

The two headed for the car as Swanson called after Holden. "Don't make yarself a pest, Holden."

"I won't Grandad," he yelled as he settled into the front seat with a huge smile on his face. As the car backed away, Holden asked in a hesitant tone, "Do you think you could swing by Archie's house and pick him up? He'd love to get a ride in this beauty."

"I can do that. You give me directions," Moore smiled.

Holden began to direct Moore, who asked, "Why does your grandfather have an iron skillet hanging from that tree limb by the river? Does he cook fish over there?"

"Alligators."

"What? He cooks alligators?"

Laughing, Holden responded, "Not yet. He'd like to. He'd use it to whack old Leatherhead if he's down by the river without his shotgun, and Leatherhead tries to snatch Shrimphead."

"Has that happened? Where he whacked Leatherhead in the head?"

"A couple of times. Leatherhead doesn't take kindly to that and skedaddles back into the river. Grandad gets mad because he doesn't have his shotgun with him."

"I bet."

"That gator and Grandad are going to battle it out one day. I'm betting on Grandad. Sometimes, you'll see that gator out in the river with its eyes and teethy snout poking out. It's watching Grandad. I think it scheming to get him and Shrimphead one day."

"I noticed your Grandad out on the river at night. What's he looking for? Leatherhead?" Moore asked as he watched the boy's reaction.

A serious look crossed Holden's face as he closed his lips tightly. He liked the newcomer but wasn't sure if he could trust him.

Moore pushed as he sensed the boy clamming up. "Holden, what's he up to?"

After a long pause, Holden turned sideways in his seat. "He's on a mission."

"What kind of mission?"

"Grandad won't share all of the details, but he's looking for something that was lost a long time ago. He doesn't quit. I try to encourage him. I've promised that he'll find it one day."

"And you don't know what it is?"

"No, but it keeps him focused. It gives him something to

do," Holden explained.

"Holden's promise, huh?" Moore asked.

"I guess you could call it that."

Moore's mind whirled as he wondered what Swanson was looking for. He hoped that Swanson would eventually get comfortable enough with him that he'd share what it was.

Ten minutes later, they drove down a dirt lane that led to a small mobile home on the bank of the Shallotte River close to Shallotte. Moore was stunned by its appearance. The dilapidated mobile home was set in a small lot filled with overgrown weeds and an accumulation of trash. A rusty car with its wheels missing was set on four concrete blocks. It looked like it had been neglected for years.

The home's paint was cracked and two of the windows had towels stuffed in them to cover the broken panes. A window air conditioner could be heard groaning as if it were sounding its death knell.

The torn screen door opened, and Flynn stepped out with a half-smile on his face. Probably eager to escape his surroundings, Moore thought as he felt sorry for the young man.

"Come on Archie. Emerson's taking us for a ride," Holden called.

Flynn ran to the car, taking a leap over the side into the back seat. "Cool wheels!" he smiled good-naturedly. "Where we off to?"

"Holden Beach," Holden answered. "Emerson hasn't driven there, and we're his tour guides," Holden beamed.

"Cool," Flynn said as he settled back in the seat to enjoy the convertible ride. "Can you get some tunes on that radio?"

"Sure Archie," Moore replied. "Holden, I'll put you in charge of that."

"Great," Holden said as he leaned forward to turn on the radio and find some beach music.

Moore followed Holden's instructions as they drove to Shallotte and picked up Holden Beach Road. Twenty minutes later, they were driving through a highly commercialized area with gift/souvenir shops, restaurants and other stores before the bridge to the island.

"That's a fun place to eat," Holden said as they drove by the Hot Buffalo. "Before you drive on the bridge, there's the Provision Company. They've got really good seafood," Holden said all-knowingly.

Moore glanced in the rear-view mirror and saw that Flynn wasn't as enthused about the restaurants as Holden. Probably didn't have the money to eat in them, Moore thought as they drove onto the tall concrete bridge over the Intracoastal Waterway.

"There're only four restaurants on Holden Island. They are all below the bridge except for the Flounder Pier," he said as Moore noticed Dock House Seafood and More, Castaways Raw Bar & Grill and Mermaid's Island Grill.

"Could you pull into the Flounder Pier parking lot for a minute?" Holden asked.

"Sure. Why?" Moore obliged.

"We have a passenger to pick up for our tour of Holden Island," Holden grinned mysteriously as he stepped out of the car and ran up the steps to the restaurant. Within minutes, he reappeared with a blushing Chloe in tow.

She was wide-eyed as she approached the car. "This is going to be fun," she exclaimed as Holden had Flynn step out of the car so that he and Chloe could sit together in the back. After they took their seats, Flynn sat in the front passenger seat.

"Everybody ready?" Moore petitioned, knowing what fun it was for teens to ride in a convertible with the top down.

"We're ready to wave," Holden replied quickly.

Moore saw in his mirror that the two teens had scrambled on top of the rear seat and were ready to wave at passersby like they were riding in a parade.

For the next thirty minutes, Moore drove the convertible and his passengers up and down the streets lined with vibrant-colored, beach homes on 10-foot-tall pilings. The homes were so close that they were virtually built on top of each other. They drove to each end of the island before returning to the Flounder Pier parking lot.

Moore noticed that Holden had slipped his arm around Chloe for the last five minutes of the ride. He also saw them exchange shy smiles and glances.

"End of the ride, kids. Who's hungry? I'll buy lunch," Moore offered.

"I can't. I have to go back to work," Chloe replied in a disappointed tone.

"Archie and I can join you," Holden replied eagerly. "You're hungry, aren't you Archie?"

"Always," Flynn answered with a large grin.

"Let's go then," Moore said as the four of them exited the vehicle and climbed the stairs to the Flounder Pier. When they entered the restaurant, they were greeted by Dottie.

"Now I think I know why Chloe disappeared," she smiled cheerfully.

"I was on my break," Chloe retorted quickly.

"You were on a date?" Dottie teased.

"No. My break," a red-faced Chloe answered as she grabbed several menus. "Can I show you to a table?" she asked as she tried to separate the three arrivees from Dottie and further embarrassing comments.

Holden and Flynn followed her to a window table while Moore hung back to talk with Dottie.

"It was innocent fun."

"I'm sure it was. I can remember those days," she said as she looked up to Moore with her deep blue eyes.

Boy, she was beautiful, Moore thought before speaking. "Nothing like young love."

"That's for sure," she smiled warmly.

"I better join them. I'm keeping you from your work. I wouldn't want Rachel to get after you."

"Oh, she's a sweetheart," Dottie responded as she resumed her work responsibilities. There was a bounce in her step after seeing the handsome reporter.

Moore headed for the table where he saw the boys reading the menu. "Lunch is on me, boys. Have you decided what to order?"

"Would a side salad be okay?" Flynn asked nervously.

It was obvious to Moore that Flynn was doing his best to be thrifty. "How about that triple burger or the seafood plate, Archie?" Moore asked.

"Really?" Flynn asked with a look of glee.

"Sure. I want to give you boys a real treat today."

The server appeared, and the boys ordered the triple cheeseburger while Moore ordered a flounder sandwich. He loved his flounder. While they chatted casually as they waited, Moore allowed his eyes to scan the ocean for signs of the *Aft Kicker*. It was nowhere to be seen. He turned his attention to the boys.

"I bet you boys have a lot of fun living here."

"We do," Holden replied. "It's a great playground for us

with the river, the Intracoastal Waterway and Holden Beach."

"Yeah. We started out fishing on the river and building rafts," Flynn explained as he finished taking a sip of his sweet tea. "Holden's grandad got us started early."

"Have you both been on the shrimp trawlers?" Moore asked.

The two boys exchanged all-knowing looks.

"Oh yeah," Flynn replied. "Hard work and long days."

"But good money," Holden added. "We're on call to help out when they are short a shrimper."

"I fully understand. I went out with them the other day. I was beat. It makes me appreciate the job I have," Moore explained as the server delivered their meals to which they all turned their attention.

After finishing their meals and paying the bill, Moore led the boys out of the restaurant for the return ride to Shallotte.

"Would you like to see the Waterway Marina on the Intracoastal Waterway?" Holden asked. "Sometimes you'll see huge yachts refueling before they continue on it."

"That's fine," Moore said as he turned in the direction that Holden pointed. Within minutes they were approaching the large marina on the waterway. "There's some big yachts there," Moore acknowledged.

"There's the *Aft Kicker*," Flynn said in an angry tone.

Moore looked and saw the Island Hopper refueling. "Friends of yours?" he asked, curious as to what the boys would say.

"They're the..." Holden started before being cut off by Flynn.

"They're not friends," Flynn grunted tersely.

"Ryan and I had a run-in with them," Moore commented, wanting to see if that would garner an explanation from the boys.

"You too!" Holden exclaimed without thinking as Flynn gave Holden a death stare.

"Yeah. They didn't like us getting too close to what they were doing. Is that what happened with you two? Is that why your gas line went missing?" Moore probed.

Seeing that Moore was putting two and two together, Flynn decided to open up. "Yeah. They had the drop on us. But there's nothing like payback. Their day will come," he declared firmly.

"You better be careful about messing with them, Archie. I've encountered people like them before. They mean business, and it isn't good business," Moore cautioned.

"They don't scare me none," Flynn boasted with foolish determination.

"I'm serious Archie," Moore reiterated. "I know their kind. Dangerous."

"Whatever," Flynn countered. He planned on finding a way to pay them back for screwing with his boat.

"Let's head back to Shallotte," Moore directed as he headed the vehicle for the bridge off the island.

Little did Moore know that the occupants of the Island Hopper saw them.

"Remember them, Derek?" Carlson asked.

"Yep, and I hope they remember to stay away from us," Binder growled icily. "Finish fueling her Carlson. We've got things to do," he added gruffly.

CHAPTER 8

Late Afternoon
Ashley's House

Moore parked the car in front of Ashley's house. He had dropped the two boys at their respective homes. As he stepped out of the convertible, his cell phone rang. "Hello?"

"Emerson?" Wilbanks asked.

"Yes, Ralph."

"Boy, y'all are not going to believe what I found here in Columbia," Wilbanks started.

"How's that?"

"I visited with my friends in the archives. The ones who focused on shipping out of Charleston. That's when I learned that the one guy who handled research on the manifests of ships during the Civil War had died recently."

"Was it due to an illness?" Moore asked, not understanding where the explanation was headed.

"No. He ran off the road in his car one night and hit a tree. That collision killed him. They said his body reeked from alcohol."

"That happens when you over-imbibe and drive," Moore responded.

"Y'all don't understand, Emerson. This guy was a Bible-thumping Christian who never had a drink in his life."

Moore was now all ears.

"And furthermore, my friend, there are some files missing from the archives."

"This is getting interesting," Moore remarked.

"And that's not all. I'm just getting started. The guy who

died, well his boss didn't show up for work the next day. His name was Don Dedmon. I knew him. He was a polecat, a real backstabber."

"He worked in the archives, too?" Moore asked.

"If y'all want to call anything he did, work," Wilbanks stated sarcastically.

"Maybe he was sick," Moore suggested.

"Nope. The family doesn't know where he is. Dedmon's boss told me that the family said he left the house for work. Nothing unusual. He just didn't make it to work. The police are involved."

"You think there's a link between the missing Dedmon and the other guy's death?" Moore questioned.

"My momma didn't raise no dummy here, Emerson. I'm sure of it. I know some of the guys down at the police station. I'm going to head over there and see if I can find out anything," Wilbanks stated firmly.

"Let me know what you find."

"I'll do that," Wilbanks said as he ended the call.

Moore sat back as he allowed his mind to process the information from Wilbanks. Was there a connection to these two incidents and the men in the Island Hopper? If there was, what was so critical that would cause the death of one man and the other to go missing? Or was Dedmon really missing? Did he see an opportunity go to work with the Island Hopper crew?

Before Moore could continue his thoughts, he was distracted by the sound of a noisy vehicle approaching him. He turned and saw Swanson at the wheel of his truck.

"Emerson, come along with me. I'll let ya help me."

"Help you do what?" Moore asked.

"Hop in. Ya will see."

Moore walked around the truck and started to open the door. It didn't budge.

"Ya have to pull hard," Swanson advised.

Moore gave it a hard pull and the door opened with a loud squeak. "It needs some TLC," Moore cracked.

"Now don't get me started with that alphabet stuff. Them BLTs or LBQ whatevers are going to be the death of me. I'm up to my ears with folks trying to tell me to be politically correct. That's an oxymoron, ya know?" Swanson jeered as he shifted the truck in gear, and they drove down the road.

"How's that Swaney?"

"How can ya use politics and correct in the same sentence? It don't work, I'm telling ya!"

Moore sensed that the man was easily worked up about anything that came close to wokeness. He decided to keep quiet and enjoy the mysterious ride. After ten minutes, Swanson drove up a narrow lane and parked next to a pink Volkswagen. Chuckling as he stepped out of the truck; he grabbed a pail with several apples in it.

"What are the apples for Swaney?" Moore asked confused.

"Ya will see. Come with me, Emerson. I'll show ya the tricks of an old man. I call it S.O.S. Smarter. Older. Saucy," Swanson said with a wink of his right eye.

"I'm not sure what you're up to, Swaney, but I bet it's no good," Moore commented good-naturedly as he followed Swanson. "Pretty desolate," he observed as he trailed Swanson through a narrow path edged by thick growth.

As they walked, Moore heard women nearby shouting playfully. When they emerged from the path, they found themselves on the bank of a lake. Several college coeds were frolicking in the water. Seeing their swimsuits on the bank, Moore realized that they were skinny-dipping.

"Those young ladies drove down by my house. They were looking for a place to swim with some privacy and I gave them directions to this one," Swanson explained. "I figured they wanted to go butt-naked," he chuckled softly.

"We should go," Moore said as he placed his hand on Swanson's arm to pull him away.

"Not quite yet," Swanson grinned slyly.

Just then, the women saw Swanson and Moore.

"Hey old man! Go away! Your friend can stay though," one of the naked women yelled as she looked from Swanson to the well-built Moore.

"I will in just a few minutes," Swanson said as he began extracting apples from the bucket and throwing them in the lake. "It's alligator feeding time," he shouted with mirth.

The women screamed and ran naked out of the water. They grabbed their swimsuits from the bank and ran down the path to where their car was parked.

Swanson got an eyeful and guffawed as they ran by him, giving him anger-filled glances. "Look at those little butts move," he smiled as he turned to see them skedaddle down the path. When he turned back to see how Moore was enjoying the show, he was disappointed. Moore was looking away.

"Dunderhead!" Swanson murmured "Ya don't need to act like a Boy Scout, ya know. Ya missed them! That last one would make a dog drool and wag its tail!"

Shaking his head from side to side, Moore retorted, "Not the kind of shenanigans that I pull." With Dottie being Swanson's daughter, he wanted to be on his best behavior – just in case.

"Well, don't that beat all," Swanson said as he led Moore

down the path. "Let's go. I know what ya need."

Moore was a bit nervous as to where this was going. "What do I need?"

"A visit to the Ho house," he snapped with an airy of mysterious glee.

Moore had a perplexed look on his face. "I'm not interested Swaney."

"What are you thinking boy?" Swanson asked with an exaggerated look of surprise on his face. "Xiu and Wei Ho are Chinese friends of mine. They make a tasty chicken and fried rice meal. What did ya think I meant?" Swanson questioned with an innocent look on his face as they reached his truck.

Moore just shook his head. Swanson was a real rascal, just like so many that had crossed Moore's path over the years.

On their way back to Ashley's house, they stopped briefly to pick up meals from the Ho family. When they returned to Shallotte Point, Swanson parked next to his house.

"Ya are welcome to come sit with me on my porch and enjoy yar meal, Emerson," he offered.

"Sounds good to me," Moore said, hoping to open a conversation with Swanson about the boys and the *Aft Kicker*.

As the day began turning into night, the two men walked over to the porch where Swanson pointed to a chair for Moore to sit on. "Ya want a beer?" he asked as he reached down to pat his dog. The Yorkie had been patiently waiting for his return. "Miss me, Shrimphead?" The dog barked three times in response.

"You wouldn't have sweet tea, would you?" Moore questioned.

"Ya aren't a beer guy?" Swanson asked in surprise.

"Not really. But I do love sweet tea."

"Don't got none, but I can get ya a glass of cold water. It will wash that rice down just like my beer will."

Swanson disappeared inside the house where Moore could hear him walking around on the squeaking floorboards. He returned within a few minutes with his beer and a glass of ice-cold water for Moore. He took the glass which looked like it hadn't been washed clean for some time and decided that he wouldn't drink anything from it. The men focused on eating their meals with occasional glances at the river where the tide was running out.

"Keep an eye out for that gator to appear. It likes to come down with the tide and nose around for my dog. It's a war between me and that gator with Shimphead's life on the line."

Moore noticed an iron skillet hanging from the trunk of the tree next to the dock. "What is that frying pan for, Swaney?" he asked to start the conversation. He remembered Holden telling him about it earlier.

"That's my just-in-case frying pan. If I'm down at the dock without my shotgun and that gator comes at me, I'll grab that frying pan and give it what for along the side of his head. While it's stunned, I'll use my knife and drive it through the top of its head. Easy-peasy." Swanson had a confident smile on his face.

"What do you think the guys on the Island Hopper are up to?" Moore probed.

"Probably wasting their time looking for a sunken ship. All of the shipwrecks around here have been identified. There aren't any others."

Moore noticed a hesitancy in Swanson's voice. He appeared reluctant to discuss it further. "Are you sure?"

"Yep."

Moore knew from the tone of the one-word response that

further conversation about shipwrecks in the area would be fruitless. "Swaney, is it okay to use your bathroom?"

"Go ahead. It's next to the kitchen."

Moore walked away and entered the shack. It was the first time that he had a chance to see if the inside rivaled the outside. It did.

The inside had a squeaky wooden floor, a stone fireplace, an old easy chair, and a worn sofa. The walls were decorated with old photos of shrimp trawlers, several fish skeletons, and three shrimp nets. There were a few empty beer cans on the kitchen sink amidst several dishes and pans waiting to be washed.

It smelled like fish, wood, mold and smoke, but in a good way. The walls were made of wood planks that had a few gaps between them. There were several lamps scattered around the room with three windows. A couple of the windows were missing screens and had dirty curtains.

As he headed for the bathroom, Moore could see the door to the bedroom was open and peeked inside. It contained an unmade bed with a sturdy chair next to it and a dresser set on two concrete blocks. After using the bathroom, Moore paused in front of the fireplace to study a long, antique oar that was affixed above the fireplace mantel. It appeared to be very old. Above the oar was a sign that read: "Dead Men Tell No Tales."

Moore returned and asked, "What's the significance of the oar on your fireplace and the sign above it?"

Swanson didn't respond.

"Swaney, I was curious about your oar and sign," Moore reiterated.

"That's private. I don't talk about it."

By the manner in which Swanson replied, Moore knew that there would be no explanation forthcoming. A car pulled up to the house and parked. They heard the door slam shut and the sound of approaching footsteps.

"Hi Dad," Dottie called as she rounded the corner. When she saw Emerson, she stopped. "Oh. I didn't know you had company."

Swaney's eyes moved quickly to her hands. He knew he was in for a treat when he saw the small foam container in her hands. "He was just getting ready to leave, weren't ya Emerson?" Swaney wasn't about to share his treat with anyone.

Taking the strong hint, Moore stood. "Yes. It's been a long day."

"I don't mean to run you off, Emerson. Dad, I brought you a piece of carrot cake from the restaurant."

"I thought that might be what ya had in that container," he smiled as she handed the container to him.

Seeing the empty fried rice and chicken containers, Dottie commented, "I see that I timed this well. Did you enjoy your dinner, Emerson?"

"It was good, but nothing like what I get at the Flounder Pier," he answered.

Swaney stood, then walked into the house to get a fork.

"I guess that's my sign to leave," Moore observed.

"Me, too. Nothing comes between my dad and carrot cake."

"I'll walk you to your car," Moore offered.

"Well, bless my heart! Aren't you the gentleman?" she exclaimed warmly as they headed to her car.

When they reached it, they paused. It was a warm evening. There was a full moon casting a silver glow on the water. The river looked like a shimmering ribbon, rippling and sparkling with every wave. It was a beautiful and peaceful moment, like a dream that one wouldn't want to end.

"Beautiful night," Moore commented as he leaned against the car fender.

"It is," Dottie agreed as she enjoyed the moment with Moore.

Moore noticed how the moonlight reflected off her blonde hair. She was absolutely beautiful, he thought. He glanced back to Swanson's place and noticed that they couldn't be seen from the porch. He decided to engage Dottie in conversation. He wanted to know her better.

"I just love that big oak tree on the riverbank," Moore began.

"It is magnificent, isn't it?" she offered demurely.

"So peaceful," Moore added.

"Magical," she said as they both turned toward each other.

Their eyes met and he felt a jolt of electricity leap between them. He wanted to wrap his arms around her and kiss her softly, allowing his warm breath to be felt on her slender neck.

She turned her head away momentarily. When she turned back, she saw him looking at her with a smile. Feeling butterflies in her stomach, she started to lean into him.

"What are ya all doing out here?" Swanson called as the bright light from his flashlight lit up the two, exposing their intimate moment and quickly extinguishing their private thoughts.

Embarrassed, they stood apart.

"Nothing, Dad!" she shouted.

"Yeah. I heard that a lot when ya started dating," Swanson yelled back. "Emerson, I don't want ya getting any ideas about taking her to Hanky Panky Cove!"

"I don't know anything about it," Moore spoke loudly.

"That's a surprise. All the teenage boys know about it," he retorted. "It's getting late and ya two should be heading home. To each of yar homes, that is," he added.

Moore was red-faced. "I guess I should go."

"Emerson, I enjoyed talking with you. You are such a gentleman," Dottie said amicably.

"I try." Too many times, I try, he thought as he turned to walk over to the Ashley house.

Swanson and Dottie talked for a few minutes before she drove the short distance home.

As she drove, she thought about Moore. He seemed like such a kind, caring man - something she wasn't used to.

Moore was thinking about her, too. He was becoming more attracted to her inner beauty. What a nice and beautiful lady, he thought. As Moore walked toward the Ashley house, he spotted Barry walking out of the Holden Seafood Company building.

"You keeping late hours?" Moore called.

"No. I had to run back. Fran left some paperwork that she needed, so I came over to get it," Barry explained.

"Good husband," Moore complimented Barry, who smiled.

"You missed some excitement on the river earlier today," Barry called as Moore walked up to the dock.

"Did that gator cause a commotion?" Moore asked.

"Nope, but you're close. It was the gator's buddy, Swaney," Barry replied.

"What happened?"

"Neville was coming downriver in his boat and Swaney was sitting at anchor in his boat, fishing. Neville came too close, and the two men started screaming at each other."

"Obviously no love lost between them," Moore mused.

"Oh, it gets better. Neville whips out his knife and cuts Swaney's fish line. That took the uproar to another level."

Moore shook his head in disbelief.

"And let me give you a word of advice. You don't want to mess with either of them. They both are skilled with those knives sheathed to their belts. They keep them as sharp as fresh razor blades," Barry cautioned Moore.

"I'll be mindful of that. You said it took the uproar to another level. What happened?"

"Then Neville shoves his throttle forward and causes a big wake. That made Swaney madder than the dickens. Swaney pulled out his knife and began waving it in Neville's direction. I heard him shouting furiously that he would get him," Barry added.

"You don't think he meant it, do you?"

"I hope not. But them two boys have been carrying a grudge for a long time. There's a real bad feeling between them two for years. It's like a threatening storm brewing between them. One day, it's going to blow up. It won't be pretty," Barry remarked with concern.

"I hope that doesn't come to pass. Think they could ever reconcile?" Moore asked.

"Doubt it. They hate each other's guts," Barry said as they ended the conversation, and Moore headed for the house.

CHAPTER 9

The Next Morning
Ashley's House

The sound of his cell phone buzzing woke Moore from his deep slumber. He picked up the phone, glancing at the time. It was 7:00 a.m. He saw that it was Wilbanks calling as he answered.

"Hello Ralph. You're up early."

"Well so would y'all if y'all go to bed with the chickens like I do," Wilbanks retorted. "Y'all ready for some interesting news?"

"Yes," Moore replied as he swung his legs over the bed and sat up. "Fire away."

"I tracked down old Mooney Harris. He's close to 100-years-old and doesn't hear as well as he used to."

"Who is Mooney Harris?"

"Mooney is a walking encyclopedia of Civil War ship knowledge. Y'all do know what an encyclopedia is, don't y'all?" Wilbanks asked in a teasing tone.

"Yes. Used them when I was a kid," Moore answered.

"Yeah. Everything these days is Google this or that," Wilbanks explained with disgust. "Mooney is kind of an interesting guy. He always had a knack for listening to old-timers and their tales. He ended up working for the South Carolina Department of Archives and History up until he retired about 25 years ago. He still gets called on to make presentations or answer questions. I stopped by Mooney's last night and spent some time with him. It cost me a bottle of rum which I'm counting on y'all reimbursing me for."

"Count on it. What did you learn?" Moore probed.

"Mooney did some work in North Carolina, too. That's part of the reason I stopped. About two hours into our visit and half a bottle of rum, he told me a little-known story. It's the legend of the ghost ship."

"Ghost ship? You think he had too much rum?" Moore asked skeptically.

"Mooney can hold his rum. During the Civil War, there was a blockade-runner that put out from Charleston. Her name was the CSS *Myrtle*. She was headed for Wilmington but never made her port. She just disappeared."

"Did Union gunboats take her out?" Moore asked.

"Don't think so. There would have been a record of her sinking," Wilbanks explained. "It could have been a storm or maybe her boilers blew up and she sunk."

"What does that have to do with these guys on the Island Hopper?" Moore asked.

"Maybe they are on to her. Trying to find her. What if they kidnapped that feller Dedmon who disappeared from Columbia to have him help find her? Maybe he's even in cahoots with them," Wilbanks suggested.

"I don't know. Everything I'm seeing or hearing here is that the Island Hopper is still running a grid," Moore replied with skepticism.

"Y'all keep your ear to the ground. If y'all hear that they are onto something, let me know. Do y'all have access to a boat up there?"

"Yes. Why?"

"Might be that Anne and I will grab some of my equipment and run up there to take a look with an underwater camera if y'all turn up something worthwhile."

"I'll do that. Thanks Ralph. I appreciate everything you've done. Are you still in Columbia?"

"Oh no. I drove back home last night. My Anne needs me," he answered in a suggestive tone.

Laughing, Moore replied, "You tell her I'll do my best to keep you two together."

"It'd take a good-sized pry bar to separate me from that sweet woman," Wilbanks joked as they ended the call.

Moore showered, shaved and walked down the hall to join Rachel and Ashley for breakfast.

"What do you have planned for today, Emerson?" Ashley asked.

"Nothing. I'll probably walk over and talk to Barry, then head for the beach."

"You can take my boat if you like," Ashley offered.

"Our boat, dear," Rachel corrected her husband in a loving tone.

"What was I thinking? Yes, of course, our boat," he smiled.

After breakfast, Moore walked over to the Holden Seafood Company building. As he walked through the door, Fran greeted him. "Morning Emerson. Ready for another trawler ride?"

"Oh no," Moore answered hurriedly. "My shrimping days are behind me."

"I didn't mean shrimping. Barry's out on the dock with Corbett. There's a problem with the trawler and Corbett is going to take it up to Southport. Ever been to Southport?"

"I haven't."

"It's up the Intracoastal Waterway where the Cape Fear River meets the Atlantic Ocean. They've got all kinds of beautiful period houses up there. And if you like live oaks like that one yonder," she said as she pointed to the live oak over Swanson's home, "you'll find the streets in Southport are lined with them."

"Sounds like a place I should visit. Do they have any waterfront restaurants?"

"Several. Now you get yourself out there and talk to Barry and Corbett about hitching a ride with them," she urged.

"I'm on my way," Moore affirmed as he walked out of the building. As he neared the trawler, Barry spotted him.

"Where have you been hiding?" Barry called.

"Probably from us. He's worried that he'll have to go shrimping with us again," Corbett teased.

"Not that I'm worried, but I just don't see shrimping in my near future. Eating shrimp is another thing," Moore said as he smacked his lips. "What's going on with the trawler?"

"The engine is running rough, and I need to get it checked out. If you're not doing anything, you're welcome to ride up to the Fraizer Marina in Southport with us," Corbett said.

"Sure. Sounds like fun."

"I can't fix this," a voice called as a figure popped up from below deck. It was Corbett's brother, Roddy.

"That's okay, Roddy. We'll let them experts at the marina figure it out," Corbett answered.

Moore saw the sweat pouring off of Roddy from working in the close quarters in the engine room. "You look hot, Roddy," Moore observed.

Before Roddy could respond, Barry interjected with a chuckle, "Roddy is always hot. Isn't that what the women say about you, son?"

"Always, Dad," Roddy said as he allowed a big grin to appear on his face.

Barry turned to Moore. "You keep an eye on him in Southport. Those women up there are itching to swarm all over this boy of mine," he said with a twinkle in his eye.

As Moore started to board the trawler, Barry grabbed him gently by the arm. "You have a minute?"

"Sure."

"Remember our conversation last night?"

Moore nodded. "About Swaney and Neville?"

"Yes. There's been a development that I don't like," Barry revealed as he lowered his voice.

"What's that?"

"I always check my surveillance cameras every morning to see what they recorded. The one pointed at our trawler picked up Swaney in his boat. He was headed across the river to Shell Point."

"That's where Neville lives," Moore exclaimed as a worried look crossed his face.

"Exactly. I watched the video, and it looks like Swaney returned about an hour later."

"Have you said anything to anyone else?" Moore asked.

"Nope. Don't have any reason to. I mention it to you since you seemed interested in Swaney and Neville," Barry murmured softly.

Wrinkling his brow as he pondered the information, Moore suggested, "Could you let me know if you hear anything else?"

"I can do that. Now you better get your tail on board. I see Corbett staring down at us from the wheelhouse."

"Oh boy. Be right there, Corbett. Thanks Barry," Moore said as he boarded the trawler and walked to the wheelhouse for the three-hour ride to Southport.

The trawler slowly made its way downriver to the Intracoastal Waterway where it travelled past Holden Island and Oak Island. Before it passed Southport and reached the Cape

Fear River, it pulled into a small harbor that was lined with waterfront restaurants like the American Fish Company, Provision Company, and Fishy Fishy Café on Yacht Basin Drive.

"Busy place," Moore observed as he saw the road crowded with traffic and pedestrians.

"It's a popular area. Several movies have been shot here," Corbett explained as he nudged the trawler into Fraizer Marina on West Brunswick Street. "That's the owner Sonny and his wife Alice," he said as he pointed to a gray-haired couple securing the lines from Roddy. "They run this marina. One of the best places in the area for repairs."

"What brings you to Southport, Corbett?" the gray-mustached Sonny asked as he looked up to Corbett who was standing next to the wheelhouse.

"Engine is running rough. Do you have time to check it out?" Corbett asked.

"Always for you and your family, Corbett," Sonny acknowledged as he leaped aboard the trawler, and the two men started for the engine room.

"Emerson, you can take a walk around town if you like. I'll call your cell phone when we're ready to go," Corbett called to Moore.

"Sounds good."

"Roddy, would you like to come to the office with me? I baked fresh blueberry muffins before I left the house this morning," Alice said to the handsome young man.

"I'm right behind you," Roddy answered as the two headed for the office.

Moore smiled. Women of all ages were attracted to the affable Roddy. He crossed Yacht Basin Drive and walked a few feet before he stopped to look at the street sign. He saw the street name was Moore. A perfect street to walk down, he decided.

He passed several beautiful older homes on the live oak tree-lined street before he entered the commercial district which was filled with people visiting the numerous stores and restaurants. The buildings in the area reminded Moore of a quaint New England village.

He stopped in the Southport Market, a huge brick store with a variety of items. He purchased a cold drink then walked a couple of blocks to Davis Street. He turned right on Davis and followed it to Bay Street where he paused for a few minutes to take in Bald Head Island and the water traffic on the Cape Fear River.

As he crossed Bay Street, he stopped quickly to avoid a truck going above the speed limit. He recognized Neville at the wheel. Neville seemed oblivious to anyone in the street as he sped down Bay Street. Strange, Moore thought as he continued crossing the street. Putting the incident in the back of his mind, he walked along the waterfront.

Hearing his stomach grumble, he walked down Bay Street to Oliver's Seafood Restaurant on the bank of the Cape Fear River. He placed a to-go order for three flounder sandwiches and took a seat where he had a view of the river while he waited.

Fifteen minutes later, he left the restaurant and headed toward Yacht Basin Drive, munching on his hot sandwich while he carried two sandwiches for his shipmates.

As he walked past the restaurants on Yacht Basin Drive, he noticed a number of boats. Then, he stopped in his tracks. Tied to one of the docks was an Island Hopper. It looked like the one that he had encountered off of Holden Beach.

Finishing his sandwich, Moore decided to take a closer look at the Island Hopper. As curiosity filled him, he placed the remaining two containers of flounder sandwiches on a bench and walked down the dock. As he neared the Island Hopper, he saw the name on the stern. It was the *Aft Kicker*.

A slightly-built man emerged from the cabin and Moore took a chance. "Dedmon!" he shouted.

The man's head snapped around to see who had called him. He didn't recognize Moore and was alarmed that someone had recognized him. He was doing his best to fly below the radar for numerous reasons.

"What?" he asked.

"I heard you were missing," Moore announced as he approached closer.

"You're mistaken," a voice grumbled from behind Moore.

Moore had been so focused on Dedmon that he didn't hear someone walk up behind him. Moore spun around and saw the man who had chased them off during their earlier encounter at sea.

"I don't know him, Derek," Dedmon said as he cringed with apparent fear.

Binder's face was contorted with anger as he glared at Moore. "I recognize you though. I ran you off once and I'm going to do it again," he threatened Moore.

"I was just curious as to what you were trying to find off of Holden Beach," Moore explained as he tried to shift the focus off of Dedmon.

"Curiosity killed the cat, right?" Binder sneered heatedly. "That's my business." Binder's eyes burned red with rage. "It's time for you to leave." There was a deadly tone to his voice.

"Need help, Derek?" Carlson asked as he emerged from the boat cabin with a shotgun in his hand.

Moore's eyes moved to the shotgun as Carlson raised it and

pointed it at Moore.

"I guess I should be on my way," Moore commented wisely.

"That would be the smart thing to do," Binder glared as Moore began walking back to the roadside. Binder turned to Dedmon. "What did he want?" he snapped.

Cowering, Dedmon responded fearfully, "I don't know. We didn't get far. He just called my name."

"Do you know him?" Binder drilled in.

"Never saw him before."

Binder turned to Carlson. "I don't want that guy nosing around this boat. Run him off if he shows his face around here again." He turned to Dedmon. "And that goes for you, too."

Carlson nodded his understanding. "Got it, Derek."

"Dedmon?" Binder snarled.

"Yes. Yes. I understand," Dedmon cowered under the menacing glare from Binder.

Meanwhile, Moore had retrieved the food containers and was heading back to the Fraizer Marina, a short distance away. His mind was spinning as he considered various scenarios as to what Binder and his crew were up to. With Dedmon as part of the crew, it had to deal with shipwrecks. What did Dedmon know that no one else knew? Questions. Questions. No answers.

When Moore arrived at the Fraizer Marina, he walked over to Corbett. "I brought you and Roddy flounder sandwiches," he said, handing the two containers to Corbett who passed one to Roddy. Roddy's fingers were stained blue/black from the blueberry muffins – or from diesel engine grease.

"Thank you. How did you like Southport?" Corbett asked as Sonny walked over to them.

"Beautiful little town. I really like all of the live oaks,"

Moore commented.

"That's part of the reason Alice and I live here. It's very picturesque," Sonny added as he watched the two men wolf down their sandwiches.

"I did have a little run-in on one of the docks," Moore began as he turned to Sonny. "Do you know who owns the *Aft Kicker*?"

Sonny laughed. "If you're talking about Derek Binder, I bet it wasn't a good experience."

"Bearded man with a scarred eye?" Moore asked.

Sonny nodded his head. "That would be Binder. Not a friendly fella. Keeps to himself. Doesn't talk much. At least he and his crewmate Carlson don't say much when they come in here for supplies or to fuel up."

"What kind of supplies do they get?"

"Just normal boat supplies…but he did come in one time and asked if I knew anything about side-scan sonars. I told him that I didn't. That's the only unusual thing he asked."

Moore knew from his past experience that side-scan sonars were used to find and image objects like shipwrecks on the ocean floor. He couldn't wait to tell Wilbanks.

"I told him about a guy in Shallotte who might be able to help him," Sonny offered.

"Would his name be Neville?" Moore guessed.

"Right," Fraizer answered in surprise. "How do you know Neville?"

Moore smiled. "I met him on Holden Island. Just briefly," Moore said without going into detail about the encounter at the Flounder Pier and the most recent minor incident along Bay Street.

"Neville's pretty good with side-scan sonar," Sonny offered.

Moore nodded his head. "Do you know anything else about this Derek Binder or that Carlson fellow?" He decided not to mention anything about Dedmon to any of these men.

"Nope. They just showed up here one day with that Island Hopper. Pay cash for everything and don't socialize with anyone," Sonny explained.

"I tried to give them some of my blueberry muffins one time when they were fueling up," Alice admitted. The men were so focused on their conversation that they hadn't seen her walk over.

She continued, "The look I got from him could kill. You'd think I was trying to rob him the way he acted. No sir. He's trouble if you're asking me."

"Thanks Alice," Moore said with appreciation.

"We're burning daylight. Sonny took care of the diesel and we're ready to head back to Shallotte Point," Corbett said, anxious to leave.

Before they left, Moore had one more question for Sonny. He really wanted to board the Island Hopper for a looksee. "Do you know if anyone spends the night on that Island Hopper?"

"Always. It's Carlson. Binder and the other fella usually spend the night somewhere around here. I don't know where. Alice, do you know?"

"I don't," Alice admitted.

"We really need to be going," Corbett urged anxiously.

They said their goodbyes and boarded the trawler. As the trawler pulled away from the marina, Moore spotted a familiar yellow truck driving down Yacht Basin Drive. It was Swaney Swanson's truck, and Swanson was at the wheel.

As the trawler headed back to the Holden Seafood Company, Moore wondered why Swanson was in Southport. He was actually surprised that wreck of a truck made it that far. Was there a connection to Neville being in Southport at the same time? Or was it just coincidence?

Moore took a seat in the stern where he became lost in his thoughts. Who was Derek Binder? Who was Carlson? What was Dedmon doing with them and what did Neville know about Binder's plans?

Moore decided that he'd spend some time on his laptop that late afternoon. It would be interesting to see if he could turn anything up on Binder or Carlson.

CHAPTER 10

Early Evening
Ashley House

After docking the trawler at the Holden Seafood Company dock, Moore excused himself and walked quickly to the Ashley house where he pulled out his laptop. In a minute, he was connected online and searching for answers. He later took a break and walked out to the porch where he spotted Ashley and took a seat next to him.

"Ryan," he started, "I found some interesting information on the guy on that Island Hopper."

"Really?" Ashley asked.

"I just spent the last hour researching him. It seems that he has a knack for stealing artifacts from museums around the globe and gold coins from shipwrecks."

"And he's not in prison?" Ashley asked in surprise.

"Apparently this Derek Binder is a slippery one to pin down. Looks like he has good alibis and a good set of lawyers. He's spent some time incarcerated but has been able to dodge the bullet on serving lengthy stays at any prison. He likes to operate with a small team so that he increases his odds of success."

"And it's easier to silence a smaller team," Ashley surmised.

"You read my mind. Coincidently, several of his gang members have turned up dead with no witnesses."

"He doesn't have to share the money from the sale of the loot," Ashley guessed. "The guy sounds like bad news."

"My thoughts, too, Ryan." Moore agreed.

"Anything on his cohort, Carlson?"

"Not really. Small time criminal. In and out of prison for

a variety of small thefts. Larceny. No reports of violence other than being involved in several fights," Moore noted.

"How do you get this information?" Ashley asked, leaning forward in his chair.

Moore smiled. "I'm a good researcher, plus I have law enforcement friends who help me when I need intel that I can't find. It's amazing what they can turn up."

"Yeah. All that cloak and dagger stuff," Ashley remarked. "What do you have planned for tonight?"

"I've wanted to talk to Neville. I saw his truck in Southport today. Could I borrow your Sea Hunt and boat over to his place?"

"Sure. No problem. Just don't take Swaney with you," Ashley joked, knowing the tension between the two.

"I'm glad you mentioned Swaney. I almost forgot. I saw his truck in Southport today, too. Kind of strange that they both would be there at the same time," Moore mused.

"Maybe they were having a reconciliation lunch together," Ashley joked.

Moore chuckled softly. "I wish. But why would they go to Southport when they could get together around here?" Moore asked.

"Because they didn't want people to see them together?" Ashley suggested.

"I don't know." Moore stood. "I think I'll head over to Shell Point and talk to Neville."

"Be safe. Take your time. I don't need the Sea Hunt tonight."

Moore walked over to the Holden Seafood Company dock and boarded the Sea Hunt. Within a minute, he eased the Sea Hunt away from the dock and headed to Neville's house on Shell Point which was 1,500 feet across the river.

The boat moved swiftly as the evening darkened. Moore was on a mission. He had a number of questions to ask Neville. As he approached the dock, he saw a boat submerged next to one side of it. It was a Boston Whaler Montauk with its lines tied to the dock cleats. Only the sunshade and a portion of the center console were above water.

Moore nudged the Sea Hunt against the other side of the dock, shut off its motor and tied up. As he stepped on the dock, he felt something under his shoe. He stepped back and bent over to pick it up. It was a drain plug, and now he knew what caused the Boston Whaler to sink.

He placed it back on the dock and wondered if Swanson pulled the drain plug in retaliation for Neville disrupting his fishing time. He was puzzled as to why Neville hadn't refloated his boat that day, assuming the sinking took place the prior night. Questions. Questions. Moore's mind was awhirl with thoughts as he climbed the hill with several live oaks to Neville's house.

As he approached the wooden structure, Moore noticed that the driveway was empty. Maybe Neville wasn't home. He walked onto the front screened porch which contained several chairs and a porch swing. The red lights that Ashley had informed him about were hanging from above the porch. Stopping at the door to the house, he knocked. There was no response. Moore knocked again as he called out Neville's name. Still, there was no response.

He then tried the door and found it to be unlocked. Casting aside any hesitation, he opened the door and walked inside the sparsely furnished, combined living and dining area. Flicking on the light switch, he saw several coastal pictures on the wall and artifacts on several shelves. Seeing nothing of interest, Moore walked into the kitchen. It had an oak floor like the rest of the house plus oak cabinets that needed replacing. It was a simple kitchen for a single man.

He next walked over to the small oak table with two chairs. There were various nautical charts spread open as if someone was studying them. The top chart had areas highlighted in yellow. As he studied it, Moore realized that the highlighted areas were those where he had seen the Island Hopper. That confirmed his suspicion that the boat had been running a grid. From the appearance of lines drawn on the chart, they weren't finished.

Moore decided to quickly check out the rest of the house, He walked into the bedroom and noticed the unmade bed, but nothing of interest. He returned to the front of the house, turning off the lights before stepping out to the porch where he saw the red lights had begun flashing. Moore smiled as he looked across the river at Swanson's house. He decided to give Swanson a reprieve for the evening.

He stooped down and unplugged the timer, then settled into one of the chairs to await Neville's return. Moore was looking forward to questioning him about his involvement with the Island Hopper and the significance of the highlighted areas on the nautical charts. He wanted to know what they were searching for.

The chirping of birds and early bright rays of the morning sun awoke Moore from his slumber. He had fallen asleep on Neville's porch and was slightly chilled by the early morning coastal air. Yawning and stretching, Moore stood and looked toward the driveway. Neville's truck was still missing.

Frustrated that he had failed in his quest to collar Neville, Moore walked down to the dock and untied the Sea Hunt lines. In minutes, he was headed back across the river to the Holden

Seafood Company dock. After securing the boat, he walked to the nearby Ashley house.

"Where have you been all night? Hot date?" Ashley teased as Moore walked onto the front porch where Ashley was enjoying a fresh cup of coffee.

"I wish. I ended up spending the night at Neville's house," Moore explained. "Out on his porch."

"Like I asked, hot date?" Ashley cracked again.

"Neville was a no-show." Moore then explained what he had found.

"First of all, it's a good thing Neville wasn't home. Walking in and snooping around like that could get a person shot," Ashley warned.

"Yeah. I know. It's that curiosity bug in me. Sometimes it just takes control." Moore explained.

"I've got one of those bugs, too. I call it the Rachel bug. Whenever she's around me, it just takes control," Ashley was filled with quips that morning. He then turned more serious. "What do you think that chart is really about?"

"I don't know, but I sure would like to find out," Moore commented. "I need to track down Neville."

"I'll tell Barry and some of the folks on Holden Island to keep an eye out for him. You can always look across the river to see if you spot his truck in the drive, too."

"I guess so." Moore sat down and updated Ashley on his conversation with Wilbanks and confrontation with Binder and Dedmon.

"So, the guy isn't missing," Ashley concluded.

"Right. It looks like he may have just abruptly taken a side job without telling his family. But I'm really curious as to what he knows." Moore looked at the early morning mist rising off the Shallotte River, then added, "I think I'll grab a catnap and get cleaned up. I probably need to make a few calls too."

"Sure. I'll leave the Sea Hunt for you. Rachel and I need to drive over to the restaurant with supplies."

"Thanks," Moore said as he turned to amble into the house to his room.

He thought about calling Wilbanks but decided it was too early. He'd call him later. The bed was calling his name. Within a moment, he was fast asleep.

CHAPTER 11

Later That Morning
Ashley House

After a short nap, Moore had shaved, showered and changed. He was sitting on the front porch with a fresh cup of coffee and a bagel as he called Wilbanks. He quickly updated Wilbanks on what had transpired in Southport with Binder and his discovering of Dedmon. He also mentioned Sonny suggesting Binder contact Neville regarding using side-scan sonar and the nautical charts he found at Neville's house.

"Y'all been busier than a cat covering its crap," Wilbanks cracked after Moore finished.

"You could say that," Moore agreed. "But I'm not sure I'm making a lot of progress," he added in a dejected tone.

"This is a difficult one to figure out. Difficult as trying to bag flies," Wilbanks admitted. "So, it looked like Dedmon was there on his own accord?"

"Yes. I didn't get a sense that he was reluctant to be there."

"I should mention it to the police, but I don't need to stick my nose in Dedmon's business. I don't really know what his situation is with his family. Maybe they are on the outs. I'll just let that sleeping cat lie." Wilbanks paused before asking, "What are y'all going to do next?"

"I'm not sure. Ryan is trying to find Neville for me so I can talk to him. He does show up at Ryan's restaurant from time to time. I could corner him there and grill him."

"The fact that Binder is asking for help with side-scan sonar really confirms that them polecats are looking for something that's sunk. Got my curiosity up, too."

"I'll try to find Neville and talk to him, then I'll let you know what I learn."

"Sounds like a plan. If y'all need Anne and me to come up there for anything, just let us know. It's so hot here in the Charleston area that my chickens are laying hard-boiled eggs," Wilbanks commented with a snicker. "It's hotter than a welder's torch on steel."

Moore laughed softly at his friend's unique knack for describing things. The two ended their call, and Moore walked down to his room to get his laptop. He brought it to the front porch and began researching Binder, Dedmon and the Holden Beach coast again to see if he could turn up anything noteworthy.

As late afternoon approached, he returned his laptop to his bedroom and decided to go to the beach to catch a few rays. He slipped into his swim gear, grabbed a beach towel, shoved a change of clothes in a small beach bag and boarded the Sea Hunt for a ride down to the Holden Island dock.

Docking the boat, he walked across the road to the beach area next to Flounder Pier and relaxed for the next few hours, enjoying the late afternoon sun and swimming in the ocean. He liked listening to the waves breaking on the beach and watching the vacationing families playing in the breakers and on the beach.

As early evening approached, Moore walked up the steps to the Flounder Pier. He was hungry for a fish dinner. Entering the restaurant, he was greeted by Chloe.

"Hello Emerson. Table for one?" the beaming teenager asked.

"In a second. I'm going to change out of my swim trunks," he answered before entering the restroom. Minutes later, he returned. "I'm ready for that table."

"Okay. I'll seat you in Dottie's section if that's okay with you?" Chloe had observed the glances that the two of them shared during his earlier visits.

"Perfect."

He followed Chloe to a window table and sat down. After reviewing the menu, he cast his eyes on the ocean horizon and saw the Island Hopper running its grid. His thoughts were interrupted by Dottie's arrival.

"Emerson. It's nice to see you," she beamed warmly.

Moore took in the radiant blonde. What a looker, he thought. "It's good seeing you, too."

Noticing his reddening skin, she continued, "It looks like somebody may have gotten a little too much sun today."

Moore smiled. "Maybe. I don't usually burn. I'm a quick tanner."

Getting down to business, she asked, "And have you decided what you'd like tonight or should I guess?"

"Your company," Moore replied without thinking. His heart took control of his mouth.

Blushing, Dottie asked, "I meant from the menu?"

"I'll take the flounder dinner. I just can't get enough of fresh flounder. Is Ryan here tonight?"

"No. He and Rachel had to run some errands. Judy is here if you'd like to talk to his mother."

"No, that's fine. Oh, and I'll take a lemonade to drink."

"Got it," she said with a coy smile. She did like this attractive gentleman a bit more than she wanted to admit.

Moore spent the rest of his time at the restaurant watching the Island Hopper and looking up information on his smart phone while enjoying his drink and meal. He had been so engrossed in his online research that the time had slipped away from him. The restaurant was nearly empty. It was almost closing time.

He noticed Dottie cleaning off a large table and piling plates on a large tray. He walked over to her. "Here, I can give you a hand," he said as he picked up the overloaded tray from the table.

"Why thank you, Emerson," she said appreciatively. "You are such a gentleman!"

"I try," Moore smiled as he followed her into the kitchen and helped her unload the tray. He spent the next hour helping her clean up, confiding he didn't have anything else to do.

As they finished, Moore asked, "Do you need a ride home? I have Ryan's boat."

"I drove, but you can walk me to my car if you like," she offered.

The two walked out of the restaurant and down the steps where she paused and looked toward the beach. Hearing the luring sound of waves rolling on the beach, she suddenly suggested, "How about a barefoot walk along the beach?"

"That sounds incredible," Moore responded eagerly as he shucked off his shoes.

They began their barefoot walk in the moonlight which cast its silver glow across the sand and shimmering waves breaking on the beach. They were laughing as they wandered into the water. When she stumbled, he reached out his hand to grab hers so she didn't fall. He didn't let go. Neither did she.

They continued their walk with the waves washing over their feet. All of the ingredients were there for a romantic night beach walk. The air was warm and breezy, carrying the scent of the ocean saltwater. They enjoyed laughing and talking softly as they walked. They turned and started to return to the pier. It was getting late.

"This has been fun, Emerson," she said as they reached the restaurant steps where they had discarded their shoes. Reluctantly, she released his hand and put her shoes on. He did the same.

"I've enjoyed it very much," Moore said in a sincere tone. "I'll walk you on over to your car as I promised," he added as he reached for her hand and gripped it tightly.

Walking through the illuminated parking lot, they reached her car where she unlocked her door. As she turned to say goodbye to Moore, he looked deeply into her eyes and smiled softly. He leaned in and pressed his lips against hers and she reciprocated willingly as she draped her arms over his broad shoulders. His hands went around her waist and held her tight.

Breaking for air, she gently pushed him back. "I'm really enjoying this moment, Emerson, but I should go."

"I've wanted to do that for so long," Moore spoke quietly.

She wrinkled her nose at him. "Me too, but I do need to go."

"Just one more," he said as he moved in without waiting for a response and the two locked lips once more.

Finishing the kiss, she playfully pushed him away again, "Now Mr. Emerson Moore, what am I ever going to do with you?"

"What do you mean?"

"I could become addicted to you," she teased.

"That would be fine with me. I have my own special Seven Step Program. I call it from zero to sixty in a flash," he offered as she opened the car door and dropped into the seat.

"You are such a flirt, Emerson Moore," she said demurely

as she looked up at him. She started the engine and drove away with a wave of her hand.

He waved back and walked across the road to the dock. In a few minutes, he was riding the Sea Hunt back to the Holden Seafood Company dock.

"What are you watching Chloe?" Judy asked as she stepped out of the restaurant, locking the door behind her.

"Nothing but two people in love," the teenager said wistfully.

"Your turn will come. Give it time. Now let's get you home," Judy said as the two walked down the steps to the parking lot.

CHAPTER 12

The Next Morning
Ashley House

Sitting on the front porch with Ashley and drinking coffee seemed like it was becoming a tradition. As the two talked, Moore's phone rang. He looked at the caller ID and saw it was Sonny Fraizer, the owner of Fraizer Marine in Southport.

"Hello Sonny," Moore answered.

"Hi Emerson. I hope you don't mind me calling you. I just got your number from Corbett," Fraizer explained.

"No problem. What's up?"

"You seemed real interested in that Island Hopper that was docked here."

"I am," Moore confirmed as he sat up in his chair. "What's going on?"

"I thought you'd be interested to know that Carlson was down here this morning. He rented some dive equipment and tanks from the dive shop Alice runs here."

"That's got my attention. Did they say where they were going diving?" Moore probed.

"No. They paid with cash and left a hefty deposit," Alice chimed in on the speaker phone.

"I'll follow up. Thanks Sonny and Alice. If you hear anything more, could you let me know?"

"We will," Sonny said as they ended the call.

"Think they found something?" Ashley asked.

"Ryan, I do." Moore next called Wilbanks who answered on the second ring.

"Emerson, y'all up already? It's not noon," Wilbanks teased.

"Give the boy a break," Anne chipped in.

"Why are y'all calling me this early? Couldn't sleep, huh?"

"Ralph, I just got a call that the guys on the Island Hopper rented dive gear and several air tanks," Moore explained.

"Y'all got my attention. They must have found something interesting to dive on," Wilbanks suggested.

"My exact thoughts."

"Y'all need to find out where they're diving without letting them know that y'all are checking them out," Wilbanks stated firmly.

"I've got a drone," Ashley offered.

Moore turned to him. "Of course you would," he smiled. "Mr. Technology!"

"That would work," Wilbanks said. "Y'all could take the GPS location and then we can do our own dive with the right coordinates. Y'all need us to come up there before things go to hell in a handbasket?"

"You have dive equipment to bring?" Moore asked.

"I've got a couple things much better than that. First, I've got Anne..."

"That's my man. He knows the right thing to say, don't you Sugar?" Anne suggested sweetly.

Wilbanks continued. "Second, I've got one of the best ROVs around. We'll send it down and see the pictures it sends back on a monitor."

"Sounds good," Moore commented eagerly.

"Do y'all have a boat we can use?"

"You can use my Sea Hunt," Ashley offered.

"That works. We'll get there as fast as small-town gossip. Y'all just be sure to get the coordinates, Ryan."

"I can do that," Ashley confirmed confidently.

"Good. I better go, Emerson. We got things to pack. We should be up there by this evening. Y'all can text me an address and where we'll be staying."

"We have room at my house," Ashley offered.

"Thanks, Ryan," Moore said appreciatively.

"Hey, no problem. This is getting real interesting."

"Got to go," Wilbanks said as he ended the call.

Moore turned to Ashley. "Where's the best place to operate that drone of yours?"

"On the roof of the restaurant. I've got a covered area up there where we can sit in a couple of chairs and operate the drone. We should get an eyeful," he stated.

An hour later, the two men were on the restaurant roof and looking out to sea where they could watch the Island Hopper three miles out. It was riding at anchor.

"Let's take a look at what they're doing," Ashley said as he launched the drone. He piloted it toward the craft, and in a short amount of time the drone flew over it.

"They're diving," Ashley said as he watched the images that the drone camera provided on the monitor.

"I wonder, Ryan, what they are diving for," Moore stated as he focused on the monitor.

"That doesn't look good."

The monitor showed Binder shaking his fist at the drone, obviously having spotted it hovering overhead. In one quick motion, he grabbed the shotgun from the deck and raised it. Simultaneously, the monitor screen went blank, and the sound of a shotgun blast echoed across the ocean.

"I guess that ends this adventure without us getting the GPS coordinates," Moore groaned with frustration.

"Don't be too sure about that. I locked them in. We have

them," Ryan smiled confidently.

"Good," Moore said with relief. "When Ralph and Anne get here, we can check it out. I'm sorry about your drone. I'll replace it," Moore added.

"Thank you. Those things happen. I won't press it with Binder as it's his word against mine. I don't need the grief," Ashley commented. "Besides, that was an old drone. I've had my eye on a nicer one," Ashley grinned.

"Sounds expensive," Moore noted.

"That's why I'm glad you're buying it!" Ashley snickered.

"It's the least I can do. After all, you're not charging me for staying at your place."

"I wouldn't be too sure about that, Emerson," Ashley teased with a raised eyebrow.

"Oh boy."

"Tomorrow, we'll see if the Island Hopper is around. If it's not, we'll know that it's probably safe to head out there and use Ralph's equipment," Ashley advised. The pair gathered up the remaining gear and returned downstairs to the restaurant.

"Let's grab some lunch," Ashley suggested after they stowed the gear in a storage area. He led Moore into the restaurant where they were seated at a window table.

"We can watch the Island Hopper on the horizon from here," Ashley explained as the server approached their table. It was Dottie.

She blushed as she saw Moore and Ashley. "Hello Emerson," she said warmly.

A huge smile appeared on Moore's face. "I guess we are sitting in the right section."

Ashley noticed the secretive glances the two exchanged. "Am I missing out on something here?" he asked perceptively.

"No. No," Dottie said quickly. A little too quickly. She took their orders and scurried away.

"So what goes, Emerson?" Ashley asked as he nodded his head toward the departing Dottie. "You two have something going on that I missed?"

Moore didn't respond right away. He then remarked, "She really seems like a nice lady."

"You're avoiding my question. Is that what you're trained to do as a reporter? I thought only politicians were trained that way," Ashley cracked as his eyes bore into Moore.

Moore looked out the window for a moment before responding. "If you're asking if there are any sparks between us, I guess you could say there's a few being exchanged."

"Sparks? I see what is on the verge of becoming a raging inferno!" Ashley observed with a huge grin.

"Ryan, she's a very nice lady," Moore said in a quiet tone.

"Okay. I get it. You're interested. Good for you. She's been alone for a long time. A lot of guys hit on her, but she's pretty particular if you ask me," Ashley espoused.

The men continued to talk about Dottie and the Island Hopper when their meals were served and throughout their lunch. Afterward, they returned to Ashley's house. Ashley had some errands to run, so he dropped off Moore at the house.

Moore planned to spend some time researching on his laptop while he waited for Wilbanks to arrive. Before he could enter the house, his plans were interrupted by shouting coming from the dock in front of Swanson's house. Moore turned to see Swanson swinging an iron skillet as he struck something out of his view.

Moore raced over to help. As he neared, he saw Swanson deliver a final blow to the head of a large alligator that slid off the bank into the river. In its mouth, it held a dog.

Swanson let lose a stream of obscenities as the gator's head disappeared below the river surface.

"Are you okay Swaney?" Moore asked as he reached Swanson's side.

"I'm okay. It's that Leatherhead. It was after my Shrimphead again," Swanson stated gruffly. His face was red from the exertion of striking the gator.

"I'm sorry about your dog," Moore offered.

Swanson roared with laughter. "Stupid gator. That was one of the stuffed dogs I use for bait. I hope he chokes on it or it gives him the runs."

Relieved, Moore offered, "That's good news."

"Lucky for Leatherhead that I was down here, and my shotgun was on the porch. I was getting ready to help the boys fix the boat. Kids. They're late."

"Kids can be like that," Moore agreed.

"Come on up to the house Emerson. Would you like a cold drink?"

"Sure."

Moore followed him to the porch where his little Yorkie was sleeping.

"Sit yarself down. I'll get yar drink," Swanson said as he disappeared inside. When he returned, he handed Moore a glass. "Fresh lemonade. It should be real sweet cuz I stirred it with my fingers," he teased as he sat next to Moore.

Moore hoped that Swanson was kidding as he took the drink. He carefully sipped it.

"Ya like it?" Swanson asked after he took a large gulp of it from his own glass.

"It's good. Very good," Moore acknowledged.

"That's good to hear because I just remembered that I forgot to wash my hands after I took a dump," Swanson guffawed. Seeing the concerned look appear on Moore's face, he added, "I'm just joshing ya, son."

"I'm glad that's the case," Moore commented as he pointed across the river to Shell Point. "You haven't noticed Neville's truck parked next to his house, have you?"

Swanson didn't look. "Ya mean the house that trauma built?" He didn't wait for a reply as he continued, "Captain Crisis isn't worth spit. I don't waste any time on that prince of roadkill."

"I wouldn't want you to hold back on your true feelings for the guy," Moore commented with a touch of sarcasm.

"Listen. The only thing I noticed about his place is that those stupid flashing red lights have been out for a couple of days. They are kind of hard to miss. He's so stupid that he probably shorted them out and got shocked doing it," Swanson mused.

Moore didn't reveal that he had disconnected the lights on his recent visit to Neville's house. "You really don't like the guy, do you?"

"When he dies, I want to give the eulogy," Swanson said as a thoughtful look crossed his face.

"I'm confused. I thought you didn't like the guy," Moore stammered.

"I don't. It'd be a pretty simple and short eulogy. Neville's dead. The world is a better place. The end." Swanson let lose a big belly laugh to punctuate his comment.

Moore chuckled despite himself. He was going to ask more questions when the arrival of two bicycles distracted him. Holden and Flynn arrived.

"Well bless my heart! Look who just came out of the shadow of their mommas' apron!" Swanson greeted the two boys.

"Hi Grandad," Holden called.

"Hi Swaney. Hello Emerson," Flynn chimed in as the two boys walked over to the porch.

Moore nodded his head in greeting.

"I thought ya two knuckleheads were going to be here this morning," Swaney groused.

"We were, Swaney, but I had a flat tire. It took me awhile to fix it. Then, Holden and I rode into town to get another gas line." Flynn held out the gas line for Swanson to see.

Noticing it wasn't brand new, Swanson asked, "Ya boys didn't steal it, did ya?"

Holden answered. "No. We found a used one cheaper at the marine store in Shallotte."

"Thrifty. I like that," Swanson commented as he stood. "Emerson, ya want to come along? We could use yar help in pulling Archie's flotsam onto the riverbank and flipping it over. I'm going to show them how to patch that hole in the bottom."

"Be glad to help," Moore said as the four started for the riverbank.

In a matter of minutes, they had the boat on shore and overturned. As Swanson had the boys follow him to his shed to get the patching material, Moore excused himself and returned to the Ashley house to research more information on his laptop.

CHAPTER 13

Early Evening
Holden Beach

"I don't see any leaks," Flynn said as he guided his repaired boat into the marina to fuel up.

The boys had spent the last hour running up and down the Intracoastal Waterway as they enjoyed the freedom that the boat gave them.

"Are you in any hurry to get back upriver?" Holden asked.

"No. Why?"

"It's just about closing time at the Flounder Pier. I need to run over there."

"Got to see that Chloe girl?" Flynn teased his friend.

Brushing off the innuendo, Holden remarked, "I just need to handle some business." He wasn't going to acknowledge Flynn was right.

"Go on. I'll finish fueling and move the boat over yonder. Then, I'll just sit back and enjoy watching the boats go by," Flynn said.

A few minutes later, Holden reached the foot of the stairs. As he started to climb them, he saw Chloe standing on the edge of the beach with her toes in the water. He quickly turned in her direction and approached her.

"Need some company?" he asked as he neared her.

Chloe tilted her head as she looked up at Holden. "I suppose that would be okay."

Holden slipped off his shoes and set them next to hers on the sand. He looked up at the stars and commented, "Sure is a nice night."

"It is," she agreed bashfully as they began to walk along the beach.

A gentle breeze caressed their faces as the breaking waves splashed their feet. The air was filled with magical electricity as the stars shined like sparkling jewels in the dark sky. The soft glow of the moon cast a shimmering glow on the tops of the waves.

Holden felt awkward. He wanted to be Chloe's boyfriend but wasn't sure how to go about it. He was too embarrassed to ask anyone for advice.

"Chloe," he stammered as he tried to get the words out of his mouth.

Chloe noticed his nervousness as she turned to face him. "Yes, Holden?"

"I was wondering about something." It was torture trying to get the words out of his mouth. His tongue wouldn't work right.

"What were you wondering?"

"Do you like me?" he blurted out.

There was a very long pause before she answered. "I guess so," she said with hesitation.

With an audible sigh of relief, Holden stated, "Yeah. I kinda like you, too."

They resumed walking. Twenty feet later, she stopped. "I better get back to the pier. My momma will be looking for me."

"Okay," Holden said as they turned and began their return. He began fumbling for the right words, then blundered nervously, "Maybe I should hold your hand so as you don't slip and fall in the water. Would that be okay? Do you think it would be okay?"

Chloe smiled and extended her hand. Holden grasped it

quickly as a gigantic smile filled his face and an extra twinkle appeared in his eyes. If he had taken time to look at Chloe, he would have seen she was smiling, too.

They walked in silence to the pier. Holden was too skittish to say anything in case she would change her mind. When they reached the pier, he reluctantly let go of her hand.

"I guess I'll see you around," he smiled anxiously as he looked up to her.

"I hope so," she said as she walked upstairs to the top step and sat. Smiling, she watched as Holden walked toward the marina to catch up with Flynn and return home.

After a few minutes, she saw a man walking quickly across the road toward one of the beachside houses. She next saw two other men chase after him and wrestle him to the ground. In horror, she saw one of the pursuers stab the man in the chest. The two men then half-dragged their victim across the street toward the Intracoastal Waterway.

Chloe had risen to her feet and without thinking stepped under one of the bright streetlights. She couldn't make out the two men dragging the third, but they spotted her under the bright light. She turned and quickly walked inside the restaurant.

She went straight to the ladies' room and sat inside one of the stalls, locking the door behind her. She began to cry as fear filled her, mixing with a wave of revulsion that was welling up in her stomach. When she finally stopped crying, she sat in silence and stared at the metal door in front of her. The sole sound was the dripping faucet at the sink. Each drip reverberated throughout the room like a clashing cymbal.

"Chloe," her mother called as she opened the door to the ladies' room. "Are you in here?"

"Yes," Chloe answered softly after a few moments.

"Come on girl. We need to finish locking up and head home."

"I'll be there in a second," she called.

"Are you all right? You don't sound like yourself," Judy said with concern.

"I'll be fine."

"I saw that Holden boy over here. I saw you two walking on the beach a while ago. Did something happen? Was he mean to you?" Judy probed.

"No. I'm okay." Chloe didn't want to share what she had witnessed. She was scared. The men certainly saw her sitting on the steps and she didn't want to get her mother involved.

A few minutes passed before she exited the ladies' room. Her mother was standing at the door with the restaurant keys in her hand. "Something's bugging you. I can tell by the look in your eyes."

"It's nothing Mom," Chloe said quietly as she followed her mother outside.

As Judy locked the door, Chloe's eyes scanned the parking lot to see if the two men were there, waiting for her. She breathed a small breath of relief when she didn't see anyone.

"I'll give you some space, honey. When you're ready to talk about it, you let me know."

Chloe nodded her head as the two women reached the car and drove away.

Meanwhile, Moore was sitting on the porch at the Ashley house, waiting for the Wilbanks to arrive. Earlier, he walked to the Holden Seafood Company dock where he looked toward Neville's house across the river. Still no sign of Neville's truck.

Ashley walked out on the porch to join Moore. "Ralph isn't here yet?"

"He texted me that they were a few minutes away, Ryan," Moore answered.

The sound of an approaching vehicle caught Moore's ear. "That might be them now."

The Ford Explorer with South Carolina plates and an enclosed trailer pulled to a stop in front of the porch. Wilbanks and his wife, Anne, stepped out of the vehicle.

"Sorry we weren't here earlier," Wilbanks started.

Before Moore could greet him, Anne jumped in. "We would have been here sooner if my Ralphie had listened to me. I'm his little helper. I'm the navigator. But noooo, he wouldn't listen when I told him I found a shortcut."

Wilbanks smiled sheepishly. "I misheard what she said. I thought she wanted to know if I had a sore butt, not if I wanted a short cut."

They all laughed.

"What's going on out here? You having a party without me?" Rachel asked as she walked out of the house and joined the group.

Laughing, Moore explained what had transpired and made introductions.

"You look tired. Would you like me to show you to your rooms?" Rachel asked.

"I hope you're not putting us in single beds. I can't be away from my Ralphie," Anne stated in a seductive tone.

"How's a full-size bed?" Rachel asked.

"Perfect. I'm just glad it's not king-size," Anne retorted. "I just love snuggling with my man!"

"Shucks, can't a man get any rest?" Wilbanks asked in a teasing tone.

"Not when he looks as good as you," Anne leered alluringly.

"Why don't you show them inside, Rachel. The guys will bring in their suitcases," Ashley suggested.

Hooking her arm with Anne's, Rachel walked her toward the door. "I can tell that you and I are going to be friends."

The two women disappeared inside as the men walked to the rear of the SUV.

"You have your gear in the trailer?" Moore asked as he looked at the trailer while Wilbanks emptied the trunk.

"Everything we need for tomorrow. I figure we can haul it to Ryan's boat in the morning. Is it close by?"

"Right over there," Ashley answered as he pointed to the nearby Holden Seafood Company dock.

"Good. That will make it easy."

CHAPTER 14

The Next Morning
Ashley House

Everyone had been sitting around the kitchen table spinning tales and talking about plans for the day when Moore's cell phone buzzed. He looked down and saw that it was Sonny Fraizer.

"I need to step out on the porch to take this call," Moore said as he excused himself. Within seconds, he answered. "Hello Sonny. What's up?"

"I don't know if you're interested in hearing this, but Alice was up the street and heard that they found a body here in Southport. Well actually, it was a bit out of town on a private road. It had been set on fire to make it difficult to identify."

"That's interesting, but why do you think I'd like to know about it."

"I saw that Island Hopper leave today. There was a morning haze and I couldn't quite make out who was boarding it. I didn't see that short man you told me about. They were all tall. I don't know. It may be nothing. I just wanted to pass it along. Southport is such a quiet town. We don't have violence like this, and that crew looked pretty mean. Really out of character to the type of people we are used to seeing."

"Thanks Sonny. I'll see what I can do from here."

They ended their call and Moore returned to the kitchen where he shared the information with the others.

"Y'all think it's Dedmon?" Wilbanks asked.

"I don't know what to think, Ralph. It may be nothing," Moore commented with a questioning look on his face.

"Sonny could be on to something. Barry and Corbett have always spoken highly about Sonny and his gut instincts. He could be on to something," Ashley explained, repeating himself.

"Maybe there is something to it Ryan," Moore responded as he wrinkled his brow.

"I can get it checked out. I have a picture of Dedmon on my cell phone. I can send it to a couple of friends of mine at the Coast Guard Station on Oak Island across from Southport. Maybe I can get them to pull over that Island Hopper y'all been telling me about and do a safety inspection at sea. They can see if Dedmon is on board," Wilbanks suggested.

"That sounds good to me," Moore replied.

"My turn to excuse myself. I'll call them and see if they are willing. They owe me a couple of favors." Wilbanks stepped out of the kitchen.

Five minutes later, he returned. "Timing is everything I tell y'all. They got a ship in the area and will have them do the safety inspection. I texted them Dedmon's picture," Wilbanks beamed as he reentered the kitchen.

"Great," Moore said. "It would be good to know if he's on board. May not be an issue, but it doesn't hurt to check."

"Right. If Dedmon isn't on board, we can give the Southport police a heads up. I could send them Dedmon's picture," Wilbanks suggested.

"You guys really think he's your missing man?" Ashley asked skeptically. "I mean, what are the odds?"

"We don't know," Moore said.

"It may be a wild goose chase," Wilbanks stated. "But it doesn't hurt to check," he added.

Ashley's phone buzzed.

"This is turning into a morning of phone calls," he said as

he answered. It was his mother, Judy.

"Do you have any idea what's up with Chloe?" Judy asked in a worried tone.

"What do you mean, Mom?"

"Ryan, she's been acting strange since last night. She was awful quiet on the ride home after closing."

"That is unusual. Chloe quiet? Can't be."

"Something's bothering her Ryan, but I have no idea. Did you or Rachel say anything to her or notice a difference in her?"

"I didn't but let me check with Rachel," Ashley said before calling to his wife in the kitchen. "Rachel, I've got Mom on the phone. She said my sister is acting strange. Did you notice anything last night with her or say anything to her?"

Rachel walked onto the porch. She had a puzzled look on her face. "No Ryan. Nothing out of the ordinary."

"Mom, Rachel isn't aware of anything. You think she might have a boyfriend problem?"

"I don't know, Ryan. I'll try to get her to open up this morning. If she doesn't, maybe you can see if you can pull anything out of her tonight at the restaurant."

"Okay," Ashley said as they talked another minute before ending the call.

"Everything okay?" Moore asked when Ashley reentered the room.

"Yeah. No problem. Just a family thing. Chloe is upset about something," he replied, trying to keep it as a nonevent. "Shall we head out to *My Rachel* and put the gear on board?"

"Sounds like a plan," Wilbanks said as the men and Anne walked out of the house.

Wilbanks, with Anne sitting next to him, drove the SUV and trailer over to the dock where Ashley and Moore waited. He parked and then opened the trailer doors to reveal the equipment they would be using.

"Whew! That looks expensive," Moore offered as he gazed at the bright yellow equipment. "What do you have there?"

Wilbanks beamed as he started to describe his pricey toy. "That's a SeaLion-2, Fishers top-of-the-line ROV." He turned to Ashley. "Ryan, that means remotely operated vehicle."

"I know," the technologically-oriented Ashley replied with his usual grin.

"Ryan will surprise you with how knowledgeable he is," Moore explained to Wilbanks.

The noise of an approaching vehicle distracted them. They turned their heads and saw Swanson pull to a stop in his battered, yellow pickup truck.

"What ya got there? Looks like a lot of whiz-bang to me," Swanson said as he eyed Wilbanks' equipment.

Before answering, Ashley introduced Swanson. "Ralph and Anne, you have the pleasure or displeasure of meeting our local curmudgeon, Swaney Swanson. Shrimp trawler captain extraordinaire."

"Looks like I've got competition in the curmudgeon department," Wilbanks cracked.

"There ain't no competition when I'm around," Swanson bellowed. "What ya got there?"

Ashley spoke first. "Ralph is a famous shipwreck hunter. He found the *Hunley* in Charleston Harbor."

"Ya don't say," Swanson said with a raised eyebrow. "Ya looking for something in this river?" he asked suspiciously.

"No. We're going off Holden Island. Due east of the Flounder Pier," Wilbanks answered.

"Ya ain't going to find anything. It's all been found. Ya just wasting your time," Swanson said in a serious tone. "And I'm wasting my time jawing with ya," he added as he shifted the truck in gear.

"You take care now," Anne called as Swanson departed, leaving a trail of dust.

"That boy has his tail up," Wilbanks cracked as he returned his attention to the ROV.

"He is a character," Moore agreed. "Tell us more about this ROV Ralph."

"It has four high-performance motors with extra thrust available through its Power Boost. That's in case you encounter heavier currents that we most likely will find off Holden Island. It's 1,000-foot-depth-rated and has 1,500 feet of cable to send back pictures from the cameras to our monitor on deck. It has front and rear facing color cameras with pan and tilt. The front camera has two, fully adjustable, 2200 lumen LED lights. The rear camera has high intensity LEDs."

"Ralphie doesn't have to dive as much with equipment like this," Anne interjected.

Wilbanks smiled. "Yeah. All I do is sit back on the deck in a comfy chair with a cold drink and watch the pictures. A lot easier than what we used to do."

"And a lot less dangerous," Anne added.

"And that cold drink is probably a little intoxicating," Ashley suggested.

"Boy, I knew that I was gonna like y'all the moment I set my eyes on y'all," Wilbanks winked.

"Rum?" Ashley guessed.

"Ryan, y'all and I are gonna be friends for a long time," Wilbanks beamed with twinkling eyes.

During the exchange, Moore focused on the equipment.

"That's the monitor, right?" he asked, pointing to a waterproof plastic case with a 15-inch screen.

"This boy must get up with the birds. He's so bright," Wilbanks teased. "That's the monitor. Next to it is a hand-held, wireless controller to manage the thrusters, cameras, and lights. The joystick controls descent and ascent as well as horizontal movement.

"Y'all can adjust picture quality and even hook this up to an external DVR recorder so that y'all have a permanent record of what we see. We'll be doing that. It also has a remote metal detector to help find metal objects."

"Sounds like it can make underwater exploration a lot easier," Moore observed.

"That is a fact. It reduces search time and the dangers and cost of diving operations."

"At least we have the GPS coordinates to take us right to the Island Hopper diving site," Moore added.

"And that's a big time saver," Wilbanks noted.

After they loaded the equipment aboard Ashley's Sea Hunt, Ashley explained, "Guys, I wish I could go with you, but I've got some business to take care of. You're in good hands with Emerson."

"Y'all are going to miss out on the fun," Wilbanks commented with a note of disappointment at hearing the news.

"I know, but business calls me." Ashley turned to Moore. "You have my number in case you need anything."

"Right. Thanks Ryan." Moore turned his attention to help setting up the equipment on the boat as Ashley walked away.

Thirty minutes later, Moore was at the helm of the Sea Hunt, piloting her down the Shallotte River toward the Atlantic Ocean. As they neared the Intracoastal Waterway, Wilbanks' cell phone buzzed.

Glancing at the caller ID, Wilbanks said, "It's the Coast Guard." Wilbanks moved to the stern to take the call. When he finished, he joined Moore and Anne at the center console.

"They pulled the *Aft Kicker* over for that safety inspection. My friend said that its crew wasn't very friendly. They were angry at being interrupted from their diving operation."

"Did they find Dedmon on board?" Moore asked urgently.

"No. There were three people aboard, but none of them was Dedmon."

"Ralphie, did they ask what they were diving for?" Anne interjected.

"They did and they said they were just practicing diving. That's hogwash if y'all ask me! Y'all don't run a grid, then start diving on a spot y'all have marked to practice diving," Wilbanks jeered.

"I agree," Moore said. After pausing, he added, "We probably shouldn't go out there if they're running a diving operation."

"That's not going to be a problem for us. They were so irritated at being inspected that they hoisted anchor and headed back toward Southport. At least that's what my Coast Guard contact said."

"That's good," Moore said with relief.

"But we will want to keep an eye peeled in case they decide to return," Wilbanks cautioned.

"Think we should notify the Southport police and send them Dedmon's photo?" Moore asked.

"Couldn't do any harm. I'll head back to the stern and give them a call," Wilbanks commented as he walked in that direction.

A few minutes later, he returned to the center console. "They were appreciative of the call. I texted them Dedmon's photo."

Moore shook his head. "This is probably a wild goose chase as far as Dedmon goes. When I encountered him on board, he didn't show any signs of being held against his will. I'm not sure that he was kidnapped."

"Y'all just don't know," Wilbanks said.

They were passing through Shallotte Inlet into the Atlantic when Moore's cell phone buzzed. He pulled it from his pocket and looked at the screen. It was Sonny Fraizer.

"Hello Sonny."

"Emerson, I've got an update for you," Fraizer started.

"What's that?"

"Do you remember me mentioning a guy named Neville? He lives down your way on Shell Point."

"Yes. I've been trying to find him for a couple of days, Sonny."

"The police found his truck. It was abandoned. The keys were still in the ignition. It had half a tank of gas although there was a rubber tube sticking out of the gas tank. Sounds like someone siphoned some gas out of it."

"That's not good."

"It was parked in the woods near where they found that burned body."

Moore's face dropped and his eyes widened. "Do they think it was Neville's body?" Moore asked as he reeled. He recalled seeing Swanson drive by in Southport and wondered if Swanson had been involved.

"They haven't identified the body. I did hear that the police are trying to figure out if it was Neville," Sonny said. "The police are making arrangements to have Neville's house searched."

"Tell Emerson that the keys were still in the truck's ignition," Alice called from the background.

"I did, Alice," Sonny replied.

Thinking more about the keys in the ignition, Moore suggested, "That would probably indicate that Neville was meeting with someone he knew."

"Could be," Sonny agreed.

"Thanks for letting me know," Moore commented appreciatively. "If you hear any more, could you call me?"

"Certainly," Sonny replied.

"This is unbelievable," Moore stated in shock as they ended their conversation.

"Something happen to a friend of yours?" Wilbanks asked as the Sea Hunt entered the Atlantic.

Moore quickly gave him a recap but didn't mention anything about seeing Swanson in Southport. He wanted to have a private conversation with Swanson about it.

"Things are heating up. It's getting hotter than a coon dog on a fresh track," Wilbanks kidded.

Both men searched the horizon for any sign of the Island Hopper, but couldn't spot it anywhere.

"I think we're good to go, Emerson," Wilbanks advised.

"I agree."

"I'm going to start setting up my equipment. Anne can give me a hand while y'all take us out to the GPS coordinates y'all have."

"I'll let you know when we get there," Moore stated as he focused on traveling to the correct location.

Fifteen minutes later, Moore cut back on the throttle. "We're here."

"Anne, why don't y'all switch places with Emerson. She can

handle the helm as well as any man."

"Better," Anne grinned as she moved forward, and Moore took her place in the stern.

"Just try to keep us in this spot. We'll be fighting the tide," Wilbanks requested.

"Gotcha," she answered as she placed her hand firmly on the throttle.

After ten minutes, the two men lowered the ROV over the side. Moore held it against the boat for a moment until Wilbanks engaged the motors to start its descent. As it dropped, the two men peered at the monitor. It didn't take long before the ROV was 30 feet above the sandy ocean bottom, transmitting a live feed from its forward camera.

"Let's see what we've got here," Wilbanks said as he maneuvered the ROV.

The ROV descended to 20 feet above the sandy and rock-strewn ocean floor. Its monitor revealed some of the rocks covered by coral. It also displayed a variety of fish swimming by, including croakers, spots, whiting, flounder and stingrays.

"I don't see anything of interest," Moore commented as he stared at the monitor.

"Not yet. Patience boy. Patience," Wilbanks suggested as he controlled the ROV.

Thirty minutes later, as the ROV maneuvered at 50 feet, an image began to appear on the screen.

"What do we have here?" Wilbanks asked as he squinted at the monitor.

The ROV moved closer to the image.

"It's a shipwreck and, by the looks of her, it's a Civil War era paddle-wheeler!" Wilbanks exclaimed.

As the ROV camera examined the paddle-wheeler, it showed

that the ship had suffered a catastrophic explosion. It was virtually blown in half.

"Boilers must have exploded," Wilbanks guessed.

"Any idea what ship she is?" Moore asked.

"Let's see if we can get to the stern," Wilbanks implored as he carefully maneuvered the ROV.

A few minutes later, the name of the ship on the stern became visible on their monitor.

"Emerson, do y'all believe in ghosts?"

"Sometimes. Why?"

"We found the ghost ship. It's the CSS *Myrtle*," Wilbanks stated proudly.

"What do you think she was carrying?" Moore asked anxiously.

"Not sure. But let's take a peek at what we can see externally, then we'll take a look inside as carefully as we can. I don't want to get hung up on any debris or jagged structures. And this is a war grave. We want to be careful and respect that."

Over the next 30 minutes, the ROV did a slow scan of the iron-clad hull from bow to stern. The far parts of the bow and stern were partially buried in five feet of sand. They were split in half, linked to the midsection by the remains atop the keel. The metal paddle wheels were askew as were the remnants of the two smokestacks. Its longboats were still secure in their places with the oars visible.

Finished with the examination of the ship exterior, Wilbanks directed the ROV carefully inside. "I'm not going to waste any time examining the engine room or crew quarters. Too much risk of the ROV getting hung up."

"Right," Moore agreed as he was glued to the monitor.

Wilbanks navigated the ROV through the open split and

inside the holds, still filled with undelivered cargo.

"Interesting," he commented as he brought the ROV to a halt.

"What is it?"

"See those open metal steamer trunks?" Wilbanks asked as he zoomed in the ROV camera on one of two steamer trunks. It was clearly illuminated under the bright ROV lights.

"Yes."

"They had locks on them. The locks are still there but hanging from the hasp. There's a pair of bolt cutters on the deck." Wilbanks edged the ROV forward to shine its light inside the steamer trunk.

"It's empty," Moore exclaimed.

"Aren't y'all the bright one?" Wilbanks offered sarcastically.

Moore ignored him. "What do you think was in there?"

Wilbanks initially didn't respond. He was moving the camera around as he explored the deck. "We may have a clue."

He had the ROV extend one of its arms and secure an item from the deck floor next to one of the opened steamer trunks. "We should know when we bring the ROV up. I don't think there's anything else to see down there."

"I can't wait to see what you found," Moore said excitedly.

As Wilbanks began navigating the ROV to the surface, he commented, "I need to report this shipwreck to the North Carolina Office of State Archaeology. They will want to investigate this wreck and identify it on their charts."

"With the two steamer trunks being empty, do you think Binder and his men took the contents?" Moore asked.

"Hard to say. But I wouldn't be surprised."

The two men chatted until the ROV surfaced. As they brought it aboard, Wilbanks released its grip on the item it retrieved. He held it up and carefully examined it.

"What do you think we have here, Ralph?" Moore inquired as he eagerly watched.

"I'd venture to say that this is an old sack that typically would hold gold coins," Wilbanks suggested cautiously.

"That looks like the sack you have in your collection at home," Anne called from the wheel.

"It does, doesn't it?"

"Gold coins, huh?" Moore surmised hopefully.

"Maybe."

"Should we have the Coast Guard stop that Island Hopper again and see if there are gold coins aboard it?" Moore asked as he tried to determine what the next step should be.

"Y'all need to slow down and think a minute. They were already pulled over once by the Coast Guard. Think they'd want to risk another pull over with gold coins aboard? What would y'all do if y'all were in their shoes?"

"I wouldn't take a chance on being boarded at sea or in port," Moore guessed.

"So what would y'all do?" Wilbanks pushed his friend.

"Toss it overboard in a sack and mark it to be brought up at a later date if I was suspicious that somebody was on to me?"

"Emerson, what kind of boat did you say those guys had?" Anne called from the helm.

"An Island Hopper. Why?"

"Does it look like that boat yonder?"

Moore saw her pointing and swung his head in that direction. "Yes. That's the boat," he acknowledged. "How long have they been there, Anne?"

"I'd guess about five minutes. I didn't think anything about them until just now."

"Think they're on to us?" Moore asked as he saw the Island Hopper begin to move away.

"Probably," Wilbanks answered as the Island Hopper sped away toward Southport.

They focused on securing the ROV as Anne pointed the Sea Hunt toward Holden Island.

Nearing Shallotte Inlet at the tip of Holden Island, Moore called Sonny Frazier on his cell phone.

"Hello Emerson," Sonny answered after seeing that it was Moore calling. "What's up?"

"Sonny, I don't want to trouble you, but I wondered about something."

"Ask away, Emerson."

"Do you know if that Island Hopper returned to its berth this afternoon?"

"I haven't seen it come in. Why?"

"I'd be interested in knowing what the mood of the occupants is. Could you take a stroll down there and text me?"

"Be glad to, Emerson. Not sure that I'm a good observer though."

"Don't let him fool you," Alice commented. "That husband of mine can read me like a book."

"More like a comic book," Sonny cracked as he laughed. "Seriously Emerson, I will give it a try."

"Thanks. I appreciate it," Moore said as they ended the call.

"Trouble?" Wilbanks asked.

"I'm not sure," Moore said as a number of suspicions raced through his mind including his growing suspicion about Swanson's involvement with Neville's disappearance. He moved to the helm. "Mind if I take the helm, Anne?"

"It's all yours. I'll just sit back here next to my handsome husband," she said flirtatiously as she plopped down on the stern seat next to Wilbanks.

As they entered the Shallotte Inlet, Moore turned to them. "How about an early dinner at the Flounder Pier? It's just down the Intracoastal Waterway a bit."

"As long as y'all are buying and they have rum," Wilbanks grinned.

"Yes, and yes to answer your questions," Moore replied as he pointed the Sea Hunt up the waterway.

CHAPTER 15

A Few Minutes Later
Intracoastal Waterway

In a few minutes, Moore guided the Sea Hunt into the marina that he used previously. He saw Holden and Flynn talking to another boater. "Hey boys, what are you doing here?" Moore called as he and Wilbanks secured the Sea Hunt lines.

The two boys walked over. Flynn was the first to speak, "Holden has girl problems. I had to bring him down in my boat."

Moore looked at Holden. "Girl problems? You and Chloe have issues?"

"Nah," Holden responded as he looked at the ground.

"Yes, he does," Flynn interjected.

"Archie, you stay out of this," Holden said in a tone that meant business.

Changing the subject, Moore asked, "How would you boys like to make twenty bucks?"

"Oh yeah," Flynn replied quickly. "That's boat gas money."

"We'd like you to keep an eye on the Sea Hunt and especially, the equipment on board while we grab a bite to eat."

"We can do that," Flynn answered for both of them.

"This nice gentleman will pay you when we get back," Moore said, pointing at Wilbanks.

"Well, aren't y'all kind with spending my money!" Wilbanks jested half-seriously.

"Just ignore him, Emerson. I get that all the time," Anne added.

"Yes, she does. Especially when it comes to spending my

money," Wilbanks bantered.

"Okay you two. Let's get some flounder," Moore directed as he led the couple to the Flounder Pier on the ocean side of the island.

When they entered the restaurant, they encountered a sullen-faced Chloe.

"Table for three?" she asked quietly.

"Perfect," Moore affirmed as they followed her to one of the tables overlooking the ocean.

After handing them menus, Chloe walked away. She didn't stop at the hostess stand. Instead, she went to the ladies' room and sat in one of the stalls. She had done this several times that day. Placing her hands on her face, she sobbed. She was terrified. She was sure that one of the men from last night had seen her standing outside the restaurant door. What if they came after her?

She felt on edge, waiting for something bad to happen. She hated herself for not being able to tell her mother what she saw, but she didn't want to involve her either. Chloe's shoulders felt weighed down as she continued sobbing with no one to confide in, to share her fear. A few minutes later, she tried to put on a stiff upper lip. She walked out of the stall and washed her face before returning to the hostess stand. It was going to be a long and difficult shift.

Meanwhile, Dottie appeared at Moore's table. "Hello, Emerson," she said sweetly.

"Hi Dottie," Moore responded before introducing his friends. "What's going on with Chloe?"

"It seems like everyone who knows her has been asking the same thing today. I don't know. I took her aside and tried to get her to open up, but she wouldn't."

"Do you think Holden had anything to do with it?" Moore probed.

"I talked with him, and he is as baffled as the rest of us. Hopefully, she'll open up tonight when she's done with hostessing," Dottie proposed. "Can I take your drink orders?"

"Rum for me," Wilbanks chimed in immediately.

"Of course, he will," Anne smiled. "I'll take one, too."

Dottie took Moore's order for a sweet tea and scurried away.

"Is she your girlfriend, Emerson?" Anne asked suggestively.

"What makes you think that, Anne?" Moore shot back.

"I saw the sparks fly between you. And they weren't sparks of anger," she teased.

"That Dottie's enough to make a male dog drool and wag its tail," Wilbanks said as he commented on Dottie's beauty as only he could.

The three engaged in a conversation about their discovery of the paddle-wheeler and what the crew of the Island Hopper were doing. There were several possibilities, but nothing that they could nail down. They were interrupted by the delivery of their drinks and soon by the delivery of their meals.

They were also interrupted when Moore's cell phone buzzed. It was Sonny Frazier.

"Emerson, I took that walk down to the Island Hopper," he started.

"How did it go?"

"I pretty much turned around within seconds of walking up to it. Binder was in a foul mood. He snapped at me to mind my own business in no uncertain terms when I asked if they needed their diving tanks refilled."

"Sorry to have put you through that, Sonny."

"No problem. Glad to help you out any time," Sonny said as they ended the call.

Moore quickly updated Ralph and Anne.

"That Binder fella is having the kind of bad day that would make y'all want to light someone's face afire, then put it out with a fork," Wilbanks cracked.

"I bet he is really upset," Moore agreed as they resumed the conversation and finished their meals.

As they began to leave the restaurant, Moore paused and inquired, "Ralph, would you two mind walking back to the marina by yourselves? I'll catch up in a few minutes."

"Trying to dodge paying them boys the twenty bucks, are y'all?" Wilbanks teased.

"No. I want to talk to Chloe," Moore replied.

"I hope you have success with her," Anne commented before following Wilbanks out the door.

"Thanks, Anne," Moore said as he looked around for Chloe. He spotted her seating a couple at a table and waited for her to return to the hostess stand.

She saw Moore start to approach her and busied herself with cleaning the stand. She wasn't in any mood to chitchat with anyone.

"Chloe?" Moore began.

"What?" she responded reluctantly.

"I notice that you don't seem yourself. That smile you're putting on your face is not genuine. Something is bugging you. Would you like to share it with me? Maybe I can help." Moore spoke with genuine concern.

Chloe didn't respond, instead picking up two menus as another couple entered the restaurant. "I can't talk now. I have work to do," she said in a formal tone.

Moore could easily see that she was miffed by his intrusion. He decided to butt out and let her family deal with it. Moore then caught up with the Wilbanks at the marina. They were talking to Flynn and Holden. Flynn had a big smile on his face as he held the twenty bucks in his hand.

"I see that Ralph paid you," Moore acknowledged as he winked at the boys.

"Oh yeah," Flynn answered.

"We kept an eye on the Sea Hunt and the gear. Nobody went near it," Holden added. Then he asked, "How's Chloe doing? Any change?"

"No change. Hopefully, she'll open up tonight to her mother," Moore remarked.

"We should cut the chitter-chatter and head back to the Holden Seafood Company dock. Anne and I need to drive home tonight. We have plans for tomorrow that we can't change," Wilbanks explained.

"No problem," Moore said. "Let's head back."

The three thanked the boys and boarded the Sea Hunt. Within minutes, they were heading down the Intracoastal Waterway to the mouth of the Shallotte River. Turning upstream into the river, Moore navigated the boat to its destination where they began loading the ROV into Wilbanks' trailer.

"Do you have a few minutes?" Moore asked Wilbanks as he looked toward Swanson's house.

"Sure. What's up?"

"I'd like you to visit with Swaney Swanson. He's Shallotte Point's version of you," Moore explained. "He stopped by when we were loading the ROV on the Sea Hunt. Remember?"

"I do. That real good-looking, intelligent guy, huh?" Wilbanks teased.

"He must be, Ralph," Anne chimed in good-naturedly as she gripped her husband's arm.

"Come on. You can leave your truck and trailer parked here," Moore urged. "He's as interesting to talk with as you are," Moore added. He really wanted to see the two of them engage in a conversation. He expected it would be entertaining.

"I guess we can take five minutes," Wilbanks commented. The three made their way over to Swanson's house where they found Swanson on his porch, sitting on a chair.

"Hey Swaney," Moore called as Swanson turned his head to see who was walking toward him.

"Emerson," he nodded. "What a ragtag couple ya are hanging out with," he called as he eyed Wilbanks and his wife.

"Good people," Moore said.

"What can I do ya for?" Swanson asked. "Did ya find anything in the ocean with that whiz-bang piece of equipment?"

"Why don't you tell him, Ralph?" Moore petitioned.

"Sure," Wilbanks said as he faced Swanson. "Swaney, we all went about three miles due east of Flounder Pier to a GPS location that Emerson provided us. We used the ROV to explore around the ocean bottom."

"Did ya find anything?" Swanson asked with a slight show of interest.

"Swaney, we did. We found a shipwreck."

"I thought all of the shipwrecks had been found around here," Swanson suggested as his interest piqued and his eyes widened.

"So did I. Years ago, I was involved with researching shipwrecks in the area, and I didn't think there were any others. That's why this one was a surprise," Wilbanks explained.

"Which ship did ya find? Were ya able to identify her?"

Swanson asked eagerly.

"It's a Civil War-era blockade runner. She's named the CSS *Myrtle*."

"Never heard of her. I just know of the others that have been identified," Swanson commented as he settled back in his chair.

"I know what y'all mean. I hadn't either. I did learn here recently that there was a ghost ship that went missing by that name."

"Interesting," Swanson remarked. "Do ya know what happened to her?"

"It looks like she blew her boilers. The ship is pretty much broke in half."

"Any idea what her cargo was?"

"I'm not certain, Swaney. Could have been a lot of stuff," Wilbanks commented without revealing the possibility of her transporting Confederate gold coins.

Swanson shook his head as he spoke. "Ya just don't know what ya will find in the ocean, especially in these parts."

Wilbanks had a pained look on his face. "My bladder is begging for mercy. It's a pee-emergency. Can I use y'all's porcelain throne?"

"Inside. It's next to the kitchen," Swanson instructed.

"Thanks," Wilbanks replied between clenched lips as he raced inside.

Anne, eyeing the dock, asked, "Do you mind if I wander down to the dock?"

"Go ahead. Go ahead," Swanson said as she began to make her way to it. "Watch for the big gator to stick it's head out of the water."

Anne's eyes widened. "Does it come out of the water by the

dock?"

"Only when he's hungry." Swanson glanced at his watch. "Looks like it's his supper time. I'd keep an eye out for him," he teased half-seriously.

Anne continued on her way with a heightened sense of awareness as Swanson chuckled.

Seeing that he was alone with Swanson, Moore decided to ask him a couple of questions. "Swaney, didn't I see you in Southport the other day?"

"I don't know what ya see or don't see," Swanson remarked as he dodged answering.

"No. Seriously Swaney. I thought I saw you in your yellow truck. It's hard to miss."

Swanson allowed a puzzled look to appear on his face as he scratched his chin. "Hmmm. Let me think here a second." He wrinkled his brow as he thought. "Ya know, I do believe I was up there to run an errand. Why do ya ask?"

"Did you know that Neville's truck was found on the outskirts of Southport?"

"Can't say that I knew. But is that a fact?"

"Yes. And not too far away, they found a body that had been burned beyond recognition," Moore added as he closely watched Swanson's face for a reaction. He didn't have to wait long.

Swanson's face broke into a huge smile and his eyes lit up. "Looks like I get to deliver that eulogy for him that I've dreamed of for years!"

Moore's inner senses diminished any thought of a connection between Swanson and Neville's death. Swanson appeared elated by the news.

"You really didn't like the guy," Moore offered.

"Nope," Swanson said with a serious demeanor.

"Nice little place y'all have here, Swaney," Wilbanks said as he stepped back on the porch. "I like your collectibles."

"It ain't much, but they please me," Swanson commented.

It was Wilbanks turn to look at his watch. "Emerson, we do need to be on the road. Anne, y'all coming?"

"Be right there," she called as she scurried back to the porch.

"Emerson, thank y'all for introducing us to Swaney here. It takes one smart polecat to know another," he grinned.

"It does, dudn't it?" Swanson said as he stood and shook hands with Wilbanks and gave Anne a hug. "Never pass up a hug with a pretty lady, I always say," he grinned.

"Swaney, thanks for letting us interrupt your porch time," Moore said before they walked back to Wilbanks' truck and trailer.

"Ya can interrupt me any time when ya bring news like ya did about Neville," Swaney called after them.

"Y'all told him that Neville died?" Wilbanks asked astonished.

"Yes, if it was Neville. I'm a pretty good reader of people and I'd say, by his reaction, he didn't do it," Moore explained.

"Sometimes Emerson, people can fool y'all. Don't ever forget that," Wilbanks cautioned as they reached his truck. Changing the topic, Wilbanks advised Moore, "I'm going to report the discovery of the *Myrtle* to the folks here in North Carolina. They'll want to dive on it and record it in their records."

"Certainly," Moore responded.

"When I get back and have some time, I'll study the videos we recorded to see if we missed anything."

"You have that sack you found?"

"Yes. It's in the trailer. I'll include it in my reporting. I'm sure I'll end up sending it to the right folks in North Carolina."

They said their farewells, and Moore watched them drive away, then returned to the Ashley house. Before entering, he heard the sounds of a vehicle coming down the road. He looked and saw it was a police car.

The car parked next to Swanson's house and two officers exited the vehicle. Moore guessed that they were there to interview Swanson about his trip to Southport to see if it was related to the missing Neville. But he wasn't sure.

CHAPTER 16

Later That Evening
Flounder Pier

"Chloe, why don't you go on outside and relax on the steps. Hannah and I will finish closing up the restaurant," Judy suggested to her daughter.

Chloe nodded her head as she walked toward the door. Her mood had not changed during her work shift. She was still sullen and fearful, breaking into tears from time to time.

"Breathe in some of that fresh ocean air. That might clear your head," her sister Hannah called as Chloe opened the door and walked outside where she fearfully paused to survey the parking lot for any danger. She was anxious to get to the relative safety of their home.

The door opened behind her, and she turned. It was Dottie. Walking over to Chloe, Dottie placed her hand on Chloe's arm. "Do you want to talk about it?" she asked in a caring tone.

Chloe shook her head negatively.

"Is it something that Holden did?"

"No," Chloe mumbled. "I'll be okay." She didn't want to talk about it.

Dottie reached her arms around Chloe and gave her a reassuring hug. "I'm available any time if you want to talk."

"Thank you," Chloe replied softly.

After squeezing Chloe tightly, Dottie released her arms from around her and walked down the steps. "I'll see you tomorrow." Dottie went to her car and drove away.

Chloe sat in silence, lost in her fleeting thoughts. She feared for her safety and that of her mother, Judy. She decided to wait next to her mother's car and walked down the nearby steps to the parking lot. When she reached the bottom, Chole heard a noise and felt her body stiffen as if she were a cat that had been spied by a large, menacing wild dog.

Chloe then felt two strong arms go around her. While she had hoped it was Holden, the young girl abruptly turned and was horrified by who she instead saw. As she opened her mouth to scream, one of Chloe's two male attackers forcefully shoved a towel into her mouth. The second attacker then bound her mouth and arms with duct tape before carrying her off across the street to the nearby waterway and a waiting boat. The men looked about to ensure no one witnessed the kidnapping and then disappeared with the girl.

One of the men carried her below deck and tied her to a chair. The other released the lines and began navigating the boat up the Intracoastal Waterway. Below deck, the man stared angrily into Chloe's eyes as he removed the gag from her mouth.

"What did you see last night?" he snarled as he loomed over her like a dark, evil-filled shadow.

With fear-filled eyes and a cold sweat on her forehead, Chloe replied nervously, "Nothing. I didn't see nothing. I mind my own business."

"I don't believe you. You had a good seat up on that dock to see what was going on below. Be straight with me," he growled in a menacing tone.

Chloe was terrified. Her heart was pounding fast like a racehorse running full out. She felt that something horribly brutal was going to happen. She tugged at her restraints but couldn't break them. She wanted to run to the safety of her mother.

"I am," she cried as her palms became sweaty. She felt a churning knot in her stomach that made her want to throw up.

"I don't believe you," the man said as he replaced the gag over her mouth. He walked above deck to stand next to the man navigating the boat.

"Did she say anything?" the man asked.

"No, but I'm sure she saw us kill him. We can't take the chance of her telling the police what she saw and identify us."

"There's no viable alternative."

"There isn't. We'll have to kill her."

Meanwhile, Judy and Hannah walked out of the restaurant, locking the door behind them.

"Where's Chloe?" Hannah asked.

Judy looked around. "I don't know. I told her to wait here." She looked toward her car parked in the darkened parking lot. "She's probably sitting on the ground next to the car."

The two women descended the stairs and walked over to the car.

"She's not here," Hannah noted as she walked curiously around the vehicle.

"I wonder where she could have gone to?" Judy offered. "Chloe? Chloe?" she called.

The two women called her name as they searched for her. They went to the beach and didn't see anyone there. Nor did they find her under the restaurant pier.

"Do you think she ran into Flynn and Holden? Maybe they took her on a boat ride?" Hannah suggested.

"She knows better than to take off without telling me. I'll call Holden's mother and have her check with Holden."

Judy called Dottie who answered right away. "Hi Judy. Is everything okay? You don't usually call this late."

"I'm trying to find Chloe. Do you know if she's with Holden?" Judy asked anxiously.

"I don't know. I'm still driving home, but I'll give him a call and call you right back," she offered.

"Please do," Judy said as she ended the call.

Two minutes later, Dottie called back. "She's not with Holden. Do you want me to turn around and come back to help you find her?"

Trying to calm herself, Judy took a deep breath. "Thanks. No. You go on home. If she shows up there, could you let me know?"

"I'd be glad to." Dottie paused before asking, "Are you sure you don't need me there?"

"Yes. I think everything will be fine. She may have seen a stray cat and followed it around the corner. But thanks for offering," she said before ending the call.

"No luck?" Hannah asked.

"No," Judy said as she unlocked the car and withdrew two flashlights. "You take one and look around, and I'll do the same. You have your cell phone on you?"

"Yes."

"Call me if you find her."

The two women split up with Hannah searching the immediate area and Judy walking toward the beach. Both called out Chloe's name as they looked for her. An hour later, the two women met at Judy's car. Neither one had been able to locate the missing teenager.

"I checked the dock where she liked to sit, but she wasn't there," Hannah offered.

"I warned her about the bull sharks over there. It's nighttime and that's prime feeding time," Judy stated anxiously.

Judy was filled with fear by her daughter's disappearance. Despair surged through her as her mind filled with panic. Where was Chloe?

"Maybe she got tired of waiting and began walking home," Hannah suggested as she tried to calm her mother's fears.

"I don't know. I did call home, but the phone wasn't answered."

"Why don't we drive to the house. With Chloe being upset the way she was, maybe she decided to take the long walk home to clear her mind," Hannah proposed hopefully.

Call it mother's intuition, but Judy was sure that something had happened to Chloe. Reluctantly, she agreed to try Hannah's suggestion. The two entered the car, and Judy slowly drove along. Both women kept a sharp lookout for Chloe as they rode home.

Fifteen minutes later, they pulled into the driveway. Judy raced into the house and found it empty. She turned to her cell phone and called Ashley, who had been sleeping. The sound of the cell phone awakened him.

"Who's calling this late, Ryan?" Rachel asked as he turned over from snuggling against her.

Looking at his phone, Ashley answered, "It's my mom."

"Why is she calling?"

"I'll have an answer for you in a few seconds," he remarked sleepily. "Hi Mom. What's up?"

"Ryan, have you seen Chloe?" she asked in a panicked tone.

Hearing the fear in her voice, Ashley became wide awake. "No. Isn't she with you?"

"No. She went outside the restaurant to wait while Hannah and I closed it. You know how strange she's been acting. I'm afraid that something happened to her." The words gushed from her mouth in a torrent.

"Is she with Holden?"

"No. I checked with Dottie, and they haven't seen her. Hannah and I searched all around the beach and the island, but we couldn't find her."

"Did you check the dock?" Ashley asked, remembering how she liked to sit there with her feet in the water.

"Hannah did, and there was no sign of her there."

"You calm down. Take a deep breath. I'll get Emerson and we'll head down to the island and look around. Call me if you hear anything, okay?"

"Yes. Should I call the police?"

"You can to alert them, but you can't file a missing persons report right away." Trying to calm his mother, Ashley added, "I'm sure she will turn up."

"Okay, but you keep me informed. I'll call the police," Judy said as they ended the call.

Ashley explained to his wife what Judy had reported.

"You want me to go with you?"

"No. I'll just take Emerson. We should find her," he said confidently.

Ashley rolled out of bed and padded down the hall to Moore's room. Knocking on the bedroom door, he called, "Emerson? Emerson, are you awake?"

"I am now," Moore moaned as he opened his eyes. "What's going on? I was just having a good dream," Moore cracked.

Ashley caught him up with what had transpired.

"Oh no!" Moore exclaimed.

"Can you go with me?"

"Ryan, give me a couple of minutes, and we can go," Moore said as he became alert to at the seriousness of the situation.

The two men quickly dressed and walked out the front door.

CHAPTER 17

A Few Minutes Later
Holden Seafood Company Dock

"We'll take the Sea Hunt down to the island. It's faster," Ashley explained as he led Moore to the dock next to the Holden Seafood Company building. They boarded the boat and departed with Ashley opening the throttle to send the craft quickly downriver.

"Ryan, do you have a surveillance camera at the restaurant?" Moore asked as they sped down the river.

"I have several cameras, but the one for the front door and parking lot went out of order a day ago. I have the new one in my truck and didn't get to install it yesterday. This is just nuts!" Ashley exclaimed in a regrettable tone.

Soon, they were heading out of Shallotte Inlet into the Atlantic.

"We're going to cruise along the beach. I've got two portable searchlights that we can shine toward the beach to see if we can spot her," Ashley said as he handed one of the lights to Moore. "Why don't you position yourself in the bow?" Ashley suggested as he eased back on the throttle.

Moore made his way forward and switched on the powerful searchlight. He aimed it at the shore as the boat slowed and made its way up the island coast.

Every few minutes, one of the men would shout Chloe's name, but there was no response. When they reached the tip of the island, they navigated through Lockwood Folly Inlet to the Intracoastal Waterway. They repeated the use of the searchlights with Moore, from time to time, directing it toward the mainland. When they reached the end of the island at the Shallotte Inlet, Ashley spun the wheel and pushed the throttle forward.

"We'll go back to the dock that I usually use when I go to the restaurant. You and I will fan out from there and see if we can locate her," Ashley directed.

Docking the craft and carrying their portable searchlights, they stepped onto the island dock as Ashley produced his cell phone. "I'm going to check in with my mother and see if she heard from Chloe." He punched in speed dial and Judy answered on the first ring.

"Did you find her?" Judy asked nervously.

"No, and it sounds like you didn't either." Ashley quickly updated her on what they had done and their next move. He promised to call her right away if they found Chloe.

"Doesn't sound good," Moore observed skeptically. "Has she disappeared like this in the past?"

"Chloe? No. She's always been level-headed. Something has really got to her for her to be acting so strangely. We're wasting time. Let's start searching," he said as he led Moore away from the dock.

Ashley stopped at the marina office and produced a key from his pocket. "I've got something that should make this a little easier." He unlocked a key box and withdrew two keys. Handing one key to Moore, he pointed to a dozen golf carts parked next to the office. "Here's the key to #8. You can use it as you drive around. I've got #6," he said as he walked over to the golf cart.

"Just like that? You have keys to golf carts?" Moore asked with surprise.

"The marina owner and I are friends. He lets me use a golf cart any time I need one," Ashley explained. "And he gets an occasional free flounder dinner at the restaurant," he added.

Moore nodded in understanding.

The two men jumped into the carts and began a search of the island from the Holden Beach Bridge to the Shallotte Inlet side of the island. When they didn't find her, they searched from the other side of the Holden Beach Bridge to the Lockwood Folly Inlet side of the island. Several hours later, the men finished their island search. As the early morning dawn chased away the darkness of night, the two men pulled over their golf carts.

"Nothing," a frustrated Moore commented.

"I called my mother, and she didn't have any news."

Moore looked at the Holden Beach Bridge, and an idea popped into his brain. "Is there a webcam on that bridge? We could see if she walked over it."

"There is. We'll go to the police station. It's right there on Rothschild Street," Ashley said as he pressed on the accelerator, causing the golf cart to leap forward.

Moore followed closely behind him. Closing the short distance to the Holden Beach Police Department, they parked the golf carts and went inside. An officer at the desk looked up. It was officer Dan West.

"Hello Ryan. We heard from your mother about Chloe missing and started looking for her," West stated with concern.

"My buddy Emerson and I have scoured the island, but we couldn't find her, Dan. Have you had any luck?"

"Not yet. We did check the video from last night for the bridge. She didn't walk across the bridge. There were only about ten cars that used the bridge that late at night. We're running down the license plates."

"We appreciate everything you do," Ryan said graciously.

"We'll be checking the webcams and surveillance cams this

morning to see what we can find."

"Be sure to check the one at the marina that we use. Chloe had a bad habit of sitting on the dock there with her feet in the water," Ryan suggested.

"That is on our list."

The police department phone rang. Holding his finger up for the two men to wait, West answered. "Holden Beach Police Department. Officer West. How can I help you?"

A serious look crossed West's face as the caller conveyed his findings. As the call ended, West said, "Thanks Tal. I'll send one of the officers over."

West placed the phone in its cradle as he looked at the two men. "We may have found Chloe. That was Tal Grissett. He's the fire chief over at Grissettown Longwood Fire and Rescue. He's on the Intracoastal Waterway in his boat, getting ready to go fishing. He spotted a body floating in the waterway."

"Is it Chloe?" a panicked Ashley asked. He feared the worst.

"He's retrieving the body now," West confirmed. "He doesn't know who it is, but said it looks like a teenage girl. It looked like a shark took a pretty big bite out of her and the body has the marks of a propeller striking it."

Ashley was aghast at the thought it was Chloe. His stomach was churning, and he felt bile rising in his throat. "Don't call my mother," he requested.

"Not until the body is retrieved and identified. Do you want to make the identification?" West asked.

"It better be me," Ashley said, shaken by the ominous possibility of the death of his younger sister.

"Why don't you go on over to the marina. Tal will meet you there," West suggested.

"Thanks Dan. We'll do that."

"I'll have officer Barb Sasz meet you there. She's on patrol."

The two men walked out of the station and drove their carts to the marina. They rode in silence as they feared the worst. When they arrived, they parked their carts and walked over to the dock where Ashley recognized Grissett. He and another man were placing a black body bag on the dock.

"Hello Ryan. Dan called me after you left the police station and explained that this might be your missing sister. I'm really sorry if this is her."

Ashley just shook his head as Grissett bent down to unzip the top part of the body bag. He felt his heart pounding and a shortness of breath as he watched the zipper being pulled open. A sense of nauseousness began to fill him as his body quivered. Grissett pulled the zipper down far enough to reveal the teenager's wet, grayish face. Ashley leaned forward to see her. "That's not her, Tal," Ashley said as he straightened with a sigh of relief.

"Any idea who it might be?" Grissett asked.

"Not a clue," Ashley replied as he took two steps back.

"I may know," officer Sasz said as she finished listening to a radio call.

"Go ahead," Grissett urged.

"We just got an alert from the Southport police. There's a family aboard a 60-foot Viking sport yacht with a missing teenager. Apparently, they were partying pretty hard with friends when they went through here on the Intracoastal Waterway before sunset. They didn't notice that their teenage daughter had disappeared until this morning when they couldn't find her. They think she may have fallen overboard, but they're not sure."

"What color hair did she have?" Grissett asked.

"Black," Sasz replied.

"This may be her. She has black hair," Grissett offered in a serious tone.

"Tal, I guess we'll be on our way. We're going to check the marina video to see if it shows Chloe," Ashley shared as his breathing resumed to normal and his pulse slowed.

"Good luck," Grissett called as he turned his attention to the police officer.

The two men walked away.

"That was close," Moore said as relief filled his face.

"Too close," Ashley agreed as they walked inside the marina. "Hi Bill," Ashley called to the marina owner Bill Witwer. "You heard about Chloe missing, right?"

"Yes. Word gets around," Witwer replied. "I figured that you'd be interested in seeing the surveillance videos for the marina from last night. I tried to save you some time. I checked them myself and didn't see her."

"You're positive?" Ashley questioned.

"Absolutely. You're welcome to take a look if you'd like. I know the police are going to look at it. They already called me."

Ashley paused before answering. "Well, I guess if you didn't see anything, then we won't," Ashley said frustrated. "Thanks for checking it, Bill."

Witwer nodded as the two men walked away.

"What next?" Moore asked as he yawned. He realized how tired he was.

"Let's go back home. I could use a strong cup of my wife's coffee to clear my mind."

"I'll go for that," Moore added as the men reached the Sea Hunt.

They boarded the boat and released its lines. While Ashley

took the helm and directed the watercraft into the waterway, Moore settled in the stern. He was asleep in no time.

CHAPTER 18

Later That Morning
Holden Seafood Company Dock

The sound of the engines shutting down and the boat bumping against the dock woke Moore. He glanced at his watch and saw it was 9:00 a.m. As the two men secured the boat and stepped onto the dock, they heard the sounds of an approaching boat. They turned to see Swanson at the helm of his boat. Holden and Flynn were on board with him.

"Where are you heading?" Ashley called.

Swanson cut back on the motors as they glided by. "Ryan, we heard about your sister missing. We're going to look for her."

"We'll find her," Holden shouted with a determined look on his face. "No one knows the water and backwaters here like Grandad," he added.

Swanson bent down. When he stood, he held his shotgun in his hand. "I'm not going gator hunting today. I'm gonna find Chloe and give whoever is involved with her being gone a real what-for," he grinned with a deadly glint in his eyes.

"Be careful," Moore advised as he watched Swanson return the weapon to the deck.

"Thanks. We appreciate it," Ashley yelled as Swanson powered up its motors and headed downriver.

Moore stared across the wide part of the river to Shell Point. "Looks like we've got some activity at Neville's house."

"Oh yeah?" Ashley asked as he turned to gaze at the house. "For some crazy reason, do you think Chloe might be there?"

"That is a crazy idea. I don't know, Ryan."

"Let's check it out."

In a minute, the men jumped back in the boat and directed it across the river to Shell Point. The boat bumped against Neville's dock as Moore stepped off and secured the lines. Ashley shut down the motor.

"Can I help you guys?" a police officer asked as he looked down on them from the hill the house sat on.

"We're looking for my sister, Chloe Harland," Ashley called up to the officer as he took in Neville's sunken boat on the other side of the dock.

"We all are. But that's not the prime reason we are here," the officer commented. "You're Ryan Ashley, right?"

"Right."

"I thought I recognized you. I'm sorry that your sister has gone missing."

"Thanks. The family appreciates everything that the police are doing to find her," Ashley stated firmly.

"What's going on with you guys here at Neville's house?" Moore questioned.

"Just following up on some other police business. Nothing that you two need to be concerned with."

The officer was being close-lipped about what they were working on with regard to Neville.

"I guess we should head back across the river," Ashley said as he restarted the motor.

Moore nodded as he took the hint and released the lines before jumping back on board. As they pulled away, Moore grumbled, "That wasn't productive."

"No, but at least we know that no stone is being left unturned in trying to find Chloe," Ashley stated.

In a short time, they reached the Holden Seafood Company

dock and secured the lines. The two men walked to the house where the sound of an approaching vehicle caused them to look toward the road. It was Dottie.

"Any news about Chloe?" she asked apprehensively as she pulled to a stop by the men.

"Nothing yet. We're still searching for her," Ashley answered.

"Have you talked to Judy?" Moore asked.

"I did. That's where I'm heading. I thought I'd spend some time with her before I head to work. She sounded frantic," Dottie explained with concern.

"You know your father, Holden and the Flynn boy just went downriver to search for her, right?" Moore asked.

"Holden did say something about that. As long as he's with his grandad, he should be safe," Dottie offered.

Moore wondered how safe the boys would really be, but didn't comment.

"Give my mom a hug from me when you see her," Ashley urged.

"I'll do that, Ryan," she said as she glanced at the handsome Moore before accelerating away.

Moore and Ashley walked to the house where Rachel had coffee waiting for them.

"No news?" she asked as she poured coffee in two cups.

"Nothing," Ashley replied as he settled wearily into one of the kitchen chairs.

Moore plopped in another chair. "We looked just about everywhere on Holden Island."

"Ryan, I talked to your mother a few minutes ago. She's a wreck. I can tell she's fearing the worst," Rachel said with deep concern.

Ashley shook his head from side to side. "I can't figure out what happened with Chloe."

Moore's phone rang. He looked down at it and saw it was Sonny Fraizer calling.

"Hello Sonny," he answered.

"Hey Emerson. I thought you'd want to know that the police identified the burnt body."

"Neville?" Moore guessed.

"No. It was some guy named Dedmon. He's from South Carolina from what I heard. They are still trying to determine where and when he was killed. They think he was killed somewhere else and then dumped and burned where they found him. No motive so far."

Moore's eyebrows raised as a surge of adrenaline raced through him.

"Emerson, I saw Dedmon when he was alive. He was on the Island Hopper with Binder and Carlson," Sonny added.

"I bet there's a connection between them and Dedmon's death. You might pass that along to the Southport police. You can give them my number, too," Moore volunteered.

"I'll do that," Fraizer agreed.

"Any news on Neville?" Moore probed.

"No. Not a peep."

"Thanks for letting me know," Moore said as he ended the call.

"That's interesting," Ashley commented.

"It is. I'm going to give Ralph a call since he was the one who told me about Dedmon," Moore offered as he walked out of the kitchen to his bedroom.

Closing the door gently, Moore sat on the edge of his bed. His mind was working quickly, processing the scattered pieces of the puzzle to Chloe's disappearance. He extracted his cell phone from his pocket and called Wilbanks.

"What are y'all up to?" Wilbanks asked when he answered the phone.

"Breaking news for you, Ralph. The Southport police identified that burnt body as being the guy you told me about. Dedmon," Moore explained.

"I'm sorry to hear that. Do they know who done it?" Wilbanks asked.

"I didn't hear, but I wouldn't be surprised if that Binder and Carlson on the Island Hopper are involved," Moore surmised.

"What about your buddy, Neville? Anything on him?"

"No. It's like he disappeared in thin air. I keep looking over toward his house across the river to see if the lights come on at night. Nada. Nothing."

"Aliens probably got him," Wilbanks teased as only he could.

Moore chuckled softly.

"I'll pass the news about Dedmon's death to the Columbia police although they may already have heard from the Southport police," Wilbanks suggested.

"Sure. Hey, have you started looking at the videos you took of the *Myrtle*?" Moore asked inquisitively.

"I started this morning. There's something amiss, but I'm not sure what it is. It's obvious, but I keep missing it," Wilbanks drawled thoughtfully.

"I bet you'll find it."

"I hope so. Y'all be safe now," Wilbanks said as they ended the call.

When Moore walked back into the kitchen, he noticed that Ashley was gone. "Where's Ryan?"

"He took the boat upriver to follow up on an idea he had about Chloe's whereabouts," Rachel affirmed.

Moore's cell phone buzzed. He looked at the screen and saw it was Sonny Fraizer calling again.

"Hi Sonny. What's up?" Moore asked.

"It may be nothing, but I know you have a lot of interest in that Island Hopper."

"I do. What's going on with it?"

"She just left her berth. It looks like she's heading for the Atlantic."

Moore thought a moment. "You didn't happen to notice if there was a blonde teenage girl on board, did you?"

"Can't say I did."

"We may have to check that out," Moore replied as his inner suspicions grew.

He looked out the window and saw the crew of the *Capt. C. L. Holden* preparing to leave its berth.

Turning to Rachel, Moore asked, "Could you call Ryan and ask him to track me down. I've got an idea as to where Chloe could be."

"Sure," Rachel answered as Moore raced out of the house to the dock.

CHAPTER 19

A Few Minutes Later
Holden Seafood Company Dock

Seeing him approach, Barry shouted, "What's all the rush about Emerson? You that excited about going shrimping today?"

"No. It's not that. Listen, your trawler is the only boat around. Could you help me find Chloe? You know she's missing, right?"

"Right. Hannah has been keeping Corbett in the loop," Barry answered knowingly.

"I think she may have been kidnapped," Moore offered.

"Kidnapped! Who would have done that?" Corbett shouted from the bow of the trawler where he had been listening.

"I think it was the folks on that Island Hopper that's been working off of Holden Beach."

"We sure can help," Barry commented in a serious tone. "If this is a kidnapping, are you armed?"

Moore's face filled with a frown. He had been running half-cocked. Not thinking things through. "No."

"That's not a problem. I've got a few rifles in the store. Hang on a minute," Barry said as he walked quickly to the building.

"No shrimping today, boys," Corbett called to Quint, Roddy and Lacey.

"That's okay with me. I'm game for a fight," Roddy said with a glint in his eyes.

Moore's cell phone rang. It was Ashley calling.

"Ryan, I think I'm on to something regarding Chloe's disappearance."

"Hold on. I've got some breaking news of my own for you."

"What's that, Ryan?"

"I just got a call from Dan West with the Holden Island police. They were checking videos and saw something that concerned them."

"What was that?"

"Remember our friends on the Island Hopper?"

Moore stood straight up as his eyes narrowed. "Yes. Tell me!"

"The video shows the boat leaving the marina on Holden Island a little after the time the restaurant closed. Then there's a large time gap before it appears on a camera video up the Intracoastal Waterway."

"Like it may have stopped somewhere to pick up a passenger?" Moore suggested as his adrenaline surged.

"That could be. We wouldn't know if the passenger boarded it willingly or not."

"My guess is kidnapped," Moore postulated.

"That's my thought, too," Ashley agreed quickly.

"I'm very focused on boarding the Island Hopper and demanding some answers."

"They're not going to like that," Ashley warned.

"At this stage, that's the least of my worries. Where are you?"

"Upriver."

"I'm getting ready to board the trawler here and go after that Island Hopper," Moore explained as Barry returned with the weapons and Moore followed him on board.

"I'll catch up to you. Heading out to the Atlantic?"

"Right."

"See you soon," Ashley said as he ended the call, and the

trawler crew cast off its lines.

Moore was taking a chance now, gambling on what his instincts were telling him. He was confident that the Island Hopper was the key to finding Chloe.

The trawler headed downriver as Moore headed to the wheelhouse, and Barry distributed rifles to the crew. Barry then joined Moore and Corbett in the wheelhouse where Moore updated them on the phone conversation with Ashley.

Moore became frustrated with how slow the trawler was moving downriver. "Punch it, Corbett."

Corbett smiled as he answered, "I've got her wide open at 8 knots."

"Trawlers aren't built for speed, Emerson," Barry added.

"When Ryan catches us, maybe Roddy can come aboard with me. Then we can fly out into the Atlantic and catch that Island Hopper," Moore suggested.

"That works," Barry agreed as the trawler continued to plow down the Shallotte River.

As they approached the Intracoastal Waterway, they spotted Ashley's Sea Hunt gaining on them. Ashley deftly cut his motor and brought the Sea Hunt next to the plodding trawler.

"I knew it wouldn't take me long to catch up to you," he greeted Moore.

"Glad that you were quick about it," Moore said as he handed two rifles to Ashley. He quickly jumped aboard as did Roddy who nestled down in the bow with one of the two rifles. Moore joined Ashley at the center console.

"Let's do it," Moore stated with determination.

The Sea Hunt eased away from the trawler before Ashley shoved the throttle forward, leaving the trawler in their wake. Soon the Sea Hunt was racing through Shallotte Inlet and into the Atlantic Ocean.

As they sped across the waves, they gained on another watercraft that was headed in the same direction.

"That's Swaney," Ashley said as he pointed to the boat.

"He must be thinking the same way we are," Moore guessed. "Holden and Flynn are aboard with him."

"I'm not real comfortable with him having them boys with him. This could get real serious fast, and those boys shouldn't be in harm's way," Ashley worried.

As the Sea Hunt passed Swanson's boat, Swanson pointed to the Island Hopper. "We'll meet you there!" he shouted over the noise from the roaring motors.

Ashley and Moore nodded their understanding.

As the two boats raced forward, a storm loomed on the horizon with a dark mass of clouds threatening to unleash their fury on the sea. The wind was picking up, stirring the waves into a frenzy of foam and spray. Rumbling thunder followed by flashes of lightning now were rapidly approaching. The air was thick with a heaviness that added additional tension to the rescue attempt.

The Island Hopper was rocking as Binder and Carlson surfaced from their dive. They rolled onto the swim platform and began to shed their scuba gear. Binder was in a foul mood. The dive had not been productive. There were no valuables below for them to bring aboard.

Carlson turned his head toward shore. "Looks like we've got company."

Binder stood on the rocking boat and looked in the direction Carlson was looking.

"Trouble," he started before unleashing a series of expletives. He recognized Ashley's boat and didn't want to deal with him or anyone else. "Get the weapons," he directed as the two men threw their dive gear to the deck.

Carlson quickly did as instructed and produced his shotgun and Binder's rifle.

"Should I pull the anchor, Derek?" a voice called from the helm.

"Yes, and be quick about it. We need to be ready to outrun those two boats," Binder snarled angrily.

"I know those boats. This one can't outrun them," the helmsman called as he retrieved the boat anchor.

"Then, we'll take care of business. When we're done with them, they'll be visiting Davey Jones' locker," Binder snapped as an evil smile appeared on his anger-filled face.

The Sea Hunt stopped about 20 feet away from the Island Hopper. As the two boats rose up and down in the stormy sea, Binder shouted, "Move on. I don't have any business with you."

"We're not interested in any treasure you found. We want the girl back," Moore shouted into the roar of the wind. He decided to use a direct approach based on his gut instinct that they had Chloe.

"I don't know what you're talking about. Bug off and leave us alone," Binder yelled back.

Swanson's boat pulled abreast of Ashley's, and Swanson cut the throttle back enough to keep him next to the Sea Hunt in the choppy waves.

Suddenly, Holden shouted from Swaney's boat, "There's Chloe."

The occupants of the two rescue boats looked where Holden pointed. They saw Chloe's head sticking out of the forward hatch.

"Don't know anything about a missing girl?" Moore

snapped sarcastically at Binder.

Binder ignored Moore. Instead, he shouted at the helmsman. "Get the girl and bring her on deck."

The helmsman disappeared for a moment inside the cabin. Suddenly a frantically screaming Chloe disappeared as the helmsman pulled her down from the open hatch and dragged her on deck. When the helmsman appeared with the struggling teenager, the men in the two rescue boats were astonished when they recognized him.

"Neville! I should have known you were involved with shady characters like these," Swanson roared with a contempt-filled face.

When they turned their attention back to Binder, they found themselves staring at Carlson's shotgun and Binder's rifle.

"I'd suggest that you all turn your boats around and head back to shore. Your business is finished here," Binder called out.

"Not without Chloe! She's my sister!" Ashley bellowed angrily.

"I'm going to give you a choice. Either you leave now and your sister is still alive. Or you force me to take a more drastic action with her," Binder directed with ominously darkening eyes like the approaching black storm clouds. A storm was on the verge of breaking, in more ways than one.

"We're not leaving!" Moore called in a tone that meant business.

"Neville!" Binder yelled, steaming like a pressure cooker about to explode.

"Yes, Derek?"

"I want you to take your knife and hold the blade against the girl's throat," Binder demanded in evil glee.

Neville seemed hesitant, although a panicking Chloe struggled to free herself from his iron-like grip.

"Neville, did you hear me?" Binder raged as his eyes burned red with fury.

"Yes," Neville said reluctantly as he withdrew his knife from its sheath. He looked at Chloe.

"Please don't! Please don't kill me," she begged fearfully as she tried to pull away.

"Derek, I didn't sign on to kill anyone," Neville countered hesitantly.

"Then I'll kill you for not obeying my order," Binder commanded in a cruel tone as he brought the barrel of his rifle to point at Neville.

Several actions happened in a flash. Neville suddenly threw his knife underhanded at Binder, thwarting Binder's aim as he pulled the trigger. At the same time, Neville pushed Chloe overboard into the ocean. Binder's bullet struck Neville in the shoulder, causing him to tumble overboard after Chloe.

From his concealment in the bow of the Sea Hunt, Roddy fired his rifle, killing Carlson. Ashley grabbed his rifle and brought it to bear on Binder, who disappeared over the other side of the boat. Within seconds, they heard the sound of a jet ski starting. Binder immediately roared away on the jet ski.

Meanwhile, Moore alertly dived into the ocean and was fighting the swells as he swam confidently to rescue Chloe from the heightening waves.

Swanson yelled to Flynn, "Take the wheel." He then jumped into the ocean to rescue Neville. His strong strokes took him quickly through the surging waves to Neville who feebly reached out to him.

Gripping him, Swanson began towing him back to his boat. "I guess I can do this for ya since ya helped save my grandson's girlfriend," Swanson grumbled as he valiantly fought the waves.

"Thanks Swaney," Neville croaked.

"Just don't let this be habit forming. And I want to warn ya, I'm not giving ya mouth-to-mouth. Understand?"

"Agreed," Neville said weakly.

They reached the boat, and Holden and Flynn helped pull the two men aboard.

At the same time, Chloe was struggling to stay afloat as waves cascaded over her head. She was waving her hands and shouting for help between gasps for air. She was weakening. Moore propelled himself through the surging waves to her side. "I've got you, Chloe," he said in a calm tone.

She immediately grabbed at him, trying to throw her arms around him for safety. Carefully, he pried her arms away while holding her securely.

"Relax, Chloe. I'll get you to the boat."

He began pulling her toward the Sea Hunt when he realized that the craft was inching closer to them. Ashley was trying to be careful in how he positioned the boat so as not to come crashing down on them.

"Catch this," Roddy called from the bow as he threw Moore a line.

Catching it, Moore allowed Roddy to pull them closer to the boat where Roddy hauled a coughing Chloe on board. He next repeated the process and helped Moore aboard.

Moore turned and looked out over the water for Binder. He saw the speeding jet ski rapidly vanish into the thick sheets of blowing rain that had arrived with the tempest of thunder and lightning. He instantly felt a surge of resolve within him that Binder would soon be found and brought to some form of justice – either at sea or in a jail cell.

"We need to get her dry before she goes into shock," Ashley said as he examined his sister's appearance.

"There's your answer," Roddy stated as he pointed to the closing trawler.

"That's one answer," Moore agreed. "But I have a ton of questions."

"First things first," Ashley said as he wheeled the Sea Hunt near the trawler, where they were able to quickly place Chloe. Barry hustled her into the galley where she could warm up and change into some dry clothes.

Seeing what Ashley did, Swanson navigated his boat close to the trawler. The boys then helped a weakened Neville transfer aboard the trawler just as the ocean swells began to deepen.

"Corbett, can you take them back to the dock and get medical aid for Neville?" Ashley shouted.

Corbett stuck his hand out of the wheelhouse to signal a thumbs up. He began turning the trawler to shore as its powerful engine attacked the rough seas. Moore watched with horror when the trawler dipped in the trough of waves and experienced a side row of 45 degrees. Slowly, the trawler righted itself and plunged forward through the incredibly steep waves.

As spray flew over Swanson's boat, he called out, "I'm taking the boys in."

Ashley yelled through the rain drumming against his boat. "Good idea. We'll see you at the dock."

Ashley turned to Roddy. "You up to taking that Island Hopper in? I don't want to leave it out here."

Grinning at the opportunity, Roddy replied, "Take me over by it and I'll bring her in."

It took some careful maneuvering for Ashley to bring the boats close to each other in the turbulent seas. They tied a line around Roddy's waist with Moore holding the other end. If Roddy missed his jump to the Island Hopper, Moore would be able to pull him back to the Sea Hunt.

With the ferocious winds and now torrential rain beating down on Roddy, he was able to successfully leap aboard, although he awkwardly rolled on the deck when he landed. He popped up and gave Ashley a thumbs up before making his way like a staggering drunkard to the helm. Within a couple of minutes, he had the boat pointed toward shore.

The Sea Hunt followed the Island Hopper at a safe distance as the two boats fought the waves. They finally made the Shallotte Inlet, crossed the Intracoastal Waterway with its calmer water and soon arrived at the Holden Seafood Company dock.

CHAPTER 20

Later
Holden Seafood Company Dock

When the Sea Hunt and Island Hopper reached the dock, they saw that the trawler was already docked. They secured the boats and ran through the rain to the Holden Seafood Company building. As they entered, they found Swanson, Holden, Flynn, Corbett and Barry sitting in the store chairs. They had changed into dry shirts and held cups of hot coffee as the rain continued to drum on the building's metal roof.

Barry greeted them. "There's some towels, and I have some dry t-shirts you can change into," he said, pointing to a stack of them.

"Where's Chloe?" Ashley asked with a worried look in his eyes.

"Fran's got her out back, giving her some dry clothes closer to her size. She should be out in a second. I called Judy and she's on her way over," Barry advised.

"Where's Neville?" Moore questioned as he saw that he wasn't with the others.

"Fran is going to take a look at that shoulder wound and bandage him up. Her paramedic training has always come in handy."

The men stopped talking when Chloe entered the room. Her worrisome countenance over the last couple of days had disappeared, replaced with a look of gratitude. She ran over to Ashley and hugged him.

"Chloe, we were so worried about you. Are you okay? Did they hurt you?" Ashley probed.

"I'm fine now. No, they didn't hurt me. I'm not sure what they were going to do because of what I saw, Ryan."

"What was that?" Ashley asked as he continued to hold his sister.

"It was terrible. When I was sitting on the restaurant steps the other night, I saw them kill a man. It was so awful," she said as her body shuddered at the recollection.

"Why didn't you say anything to Mom or me?" Ashley pushed.

"I was scared. I didn't know what to do. I was hoping they hadn't seen me sitting on the steps, but they did."

"You should have confided in someone," Moore interjected.

"I made a mistake," Chloe replied with her eyes downcast.

"We all do," Moore commented, trying to ease her mind.

"How did they kidnap you?" Ashley asked.

"I was down by the car the next night, waiting for Mom to finish up. They sneaked up on me. The next thing I knew, I had a gag stuffed in my mouth and they were carrying me to their boat on the Intracoastal Waterway."

Ashley gave Moore a nod, confirming their earlier suspicions.

"Did they keep you on the boat?" Ashley asked.

"Yes. They had me tied up in the cabin. I tried to get loose but couldn't."

"Did you have any idea what they were going to do with you?" Ashley probed again.

"I was worried. The tall man was really mean looking. He and the other guy would talk low so that I couldn't hear them. I knew they were talking about me, but I don't know what they were saying."

Fran and Neville then entered the room. Neville's left arm

was in a sling. He was greeted by silent stares as he scanned the people sitting there. His troubled eyes locked on Swanson. There was an electrical storm brewing inside the room. The air felt charged as an unsettling quiet descended.

No one spoke for several moments, then Swanson broke the tension.

"I guess ya and I are the two elephants in the room," Swanson started.

Neville eyed Swanson carefully. His body tensed, ready for a physical confrontation with his long-time nemesis.

"I'd believe that to be true," Neville said slowly as he watched Swanson closely.

Swanson stood to his feet and began walking toward Neville. To everyone's surprise, there was a softness in Swanson's demeanor as he approached Neville. He held out his hand and a reluctant Neville shook it.

"Ya and me have been carrying a grudge for a lot of years. I'm willing to set them ill feelings aside if ya are willing."

As the two men shook hands, a dumbfounded Neville asked, "And the reason why you are willing to let bygones be forgotten?"

"I saw what ya did out there for my grandson, not killing his girlfriend and pushing her overboard to get her away from them mad men. That's why I'm willing to let the past be in the past," Swanson explained.

Neville relaxed, allowing a smile to cross his face. "Swaney, you got a deal," he said cautiously as Swanson returned to his chair.

"Just don't be counting on me jumping into water to save yar butt all of the time," Swanson teased.

The room laughed as Roddy stepped forward. "I guess it's

safe to return your knife to you," he said as he handed Neville's knife back. "I found it on the deck of that Island Hopper."

"I'm curious, Neville. How did you get hooked up with Binder and Carlson?" Moore inquired as Neville returned the knife to its scabbard.

"They needed somebody to help run the side-scan sonar and man the helm while they were diving. They asked around and heard I was good at both. Then they contacted me," he explained. "I didn't sign on for anything else," he added.

"What about that other guy who worked for them? His name was Dedmon," Moore quizzed Neville.

"I don't know anything about him. He left after I started to work for them. That Carlson fella borrowed my truck to take him to a bus station, then he said my truck was stolen."

"Dedmon was murdered," Moore announced to Neville.

"I didn't have anything to do with that," Neville replied quickly as a look of concern appeared on his face.

"They may have been trying to frame you, Neville," Moore suggested as he recalled a conversation he had with Alice Fraizer. "A Southport friend of mine learned that your fingerprints and Dedmon's were the only ones found in the truck."

"Like I said, I didn't have anything to do with that guy," Neville spoke staunchly. He was becoming more uncomfortable about his decision to work on the Island Hopper.

"Why didn't you do something when you saw Chloe tied up?" It was Ashley's turn to ask a question.

"I'd seen her working at the Flounder Pier, but I didn't know who she was. They said it was Binder's stepchild and she was a runaway. I didn't ask anything else about her," Neville explained.

"Did you stay on board at night with her?" Moore asked.

"Yes. They wanted me to keep an eye on her."

"Where did they stay?"

"I'm not sure, but it was within walking distance because they didn't have a vehicle parked at the marina in Southport," Neville responded.

"We should call the police Emerson, and let them know what's going on, plus that we found Chloe," Ashley urged.

"Let's hold off on that for at least a few hours. I've got a couple of ideas," Moore replied. "I'm going to step outside for a moment to make a call," Emerson stated to the group. He stood from his chair and stepped onto the covered entryway to the building.

As he called Sonny Fraizer, he noticed that the rain was easing a bit.

"Hey Emerson. You got rainy weather down there like we have up here?" Fraizer asked.

"Looks like it's slowing down."

"What can I do you for?"

"Sonny, do you know where the crew from that Island Hopper are staying? Do they have a rented cottage?"

"I don't know, but I'll ask Alice. If she doesn't know, it won't take her long to find out. By the way, that Island Hopper isn't at her dock. I hope they're not out in this weather. The seas can get pretty nasty in storms like this."

"The Island Hopper is here at Shallotte Point. Get back to me as soon as you can," Moore requested urgently.

"What's the big rush?"

"I'll explain later," Moore said as he ended the call. When Moore walked back inside, he turned to Ashley. "The rainfall is lessening. Ryan, could we take your boat up to Southport?"

"Going after Binder?"

"Yes."

"Do you want some of us to come with you?" Barry asked.

"Especially me since I took out that other fellow on the Island Hopper," Roddy offered, excited to join the chase.

"No, but thanks for offering. It's only Binder now. I think Ryan and I can handle him."

"Emerson, let's run next door. I've got some rain gear we can slip into, and I'll grab a couple of my handguns and AR-15s to take with us."

"Nothing like some firepower," Moore commented.

"Overpower them, I always say," Ashley replied as they headed next door.

Within fifteen minutes, they were back on board the Sea Hunt and moving through the light rain to the Intracoastal Waterway.

CHAPTER 21

Fraizer Marina
Southport

"There's Binder's jet ski," Moore exclaimed as Ashley cut the throttle and the Sea Hunt glided toward the Fraizer Marina docks.

"He can't be far from it," Ashley surmised as he wheeled the craft next to one of the marina docks. While Ashley cut the engine, Moore secured the lines. The two men then walked inside the marina office.

"I didn't know you were coming up here on a dreary evening like this," Sonny started.

"We have some unfinished business," Moore replied. "Any news on where Binder is staying?"

"Perfect timing. Alice just got off the phone. She had to make several calls, but finally found which cottage he's renting. Alice, come on out. Emerson and Ryan are here," Sonny called.

Alice walked into the office. "You two men shouldn't be out boating in weather like this," she warned.

"It's pretty important," Moore stated. "Where's Binder staying?" he asked as he cut to the chase.

"He's nearby. On West Moore Street." She handed Moore a piece of paper. "I wrote down the address for you. It's not far from here at all."

"Thanks. We'll tell you more about what's going on when we get back," Moore said, seeing the bewildered look on the Fraziers' faces.

"We're patient," Sonny called as the two men turned and walked outside.

They went to the Sea Hunt and grabbed the AR-15s. Both were packing Smith and Wesson .38s around their waists under their rain gear. They next turned and walked the short distance to Binder's cottage.

It began to rain hard again, and it was just after 10:00 p.m. when the two men reached the cottage. Dressed in black rain jackets with black ball caps pulled down across their foreheads, the two crouched in the shadows as the dark clouds thundered overhead.

"Looks quiet," Ashley observed.

"Quiet and dangerous," Moore added as he peered toward the two-story cottage at the end of the short driveway while he gripped his AR-15 tightly.

A sudden flash of lightning illuminated the tree-shrouded cottage. The front porch light was on as were several lights inside on the first floor. It appeared that a spotlight tried to illuminate the backyard. It was having a tough time due to the sheets of falling rain. An SUV with its motor running was parked near the rear of the house.

"Looks like somebody is planning on leaving," Ashley said as water dripped off his jacket.

"That's not going to happen, Ryan. You cover the porch and I'll ease up along the side of the house," Moore instructed his friend. "I'll go through the back door while you cover the front."

"Gotcha," Ashley replied as he moved to a position closer to the front porch.

Meanwhile, Moore skirted the shrub-lined driveway, allowing the rain to help keep him in the shadows. He carefully made his way to the parked SUV. Standing from his crouched position, Moore looked through the vehicle windows. It was empty.

He cautiously walked around the rear of the vehicle to study his next move.

He watched through the cottage windows for any movement but didn't see any. He noticed that the rear door was slightly ajar. Carrying his AR-15 at waist level, Moore sprinted across the driveway to the corner of the house.

He waited, listening for any noise that would signal movement from inside. Hearing none, he moved around the corner. Using the barrel of his AR-15, he pushed the rear door open. It creaked noisily as it swung, making Moore grimace at the announcement of his arrival.

He listened again. Hearing nothing other than the thunder overhead and the sound of the raindrops striking the cottage metal roof, Moore stepped inside. The wooden floor emitted a loud squeak and suddenly the lights in the cottage went out. Moore wasn't sure if the power went out or if someone threw the switch in the breaker box.

He looked outside and saw the neighbor's house still had its lights on. It must be the breaker box, and Binder now knows the house has an intruder, Moore deduced. Since the cottage didn't have a basement, Moore guessed that breaker box was on the first level. He'd have to be careful as he walked through the house.

With his breathing rate increasing rapidly, Moore moved cautiously through the kitchen, frustrated by the squeaky floor signaling his footsteps. He looked around the sparsely furnished kitchen. There were no hiding places. Moore went as quietly as he could through the archway into the front room. He paused as he carefully scanned the dark room.

Instantly, a flash of lightning showed the silhouette of a figure sitting in a rocking chair near the front window. The figure was holding a shotgun across its lap. Moore stepped forward with his weapon leveled at the figure. "Drop the gun," Moore commanded as he stepped boldly in front of the figure. When the figure didn't respond, Moore switched on the LED head lamp clipped to the brim of his cap. He was stunned by what he saw, becoming cold from the horror.

Sitting in the rocking chair was an elderly man. He appeared to have been dead for several days. The eyes stared blankly, and blood stains covered the corpse's chest. Moore wondered if it was the cottage owner or one of Binder's henchmen.

Reaching up to switch off his light, Moore was stopped by a cruel voice calling out. "I'd suggest you put down your weapon, Moore."

Moore complied with Binder's instructions. He placed his AR-15 on the floor as he turned to the stairwell to the second floor. His light illuminated Binder sitting on the stairs. He held a shotgun in his hands that was aimed at Moore's midsection.

"Are you alone?" Binder snapped sharply.

"Yes," Moore answered, not wanting to reveal that Ashley was somewhere in front of the house.

"Of course, you would be. That's how cocksure you are about your prowess," Binder cackled gleefully. "I did some research on you. I'm well aware of your skills, so don't try to pull any tricks on me."

Moore wanted to buy time to allow Ashley to approach the house. "So what's this all about, Binder? I studied you, too. I know you've been involved in all kinds of criminal schemes. What did you find on the *Myrtle*?"

"I'm impressed. You have been putting the pieces of the puzzle together more than I thought. Simply, gold coins."

"You used Dedmon to find the shipwreck and its gold coins,

then killed him?" Moore probed.

"Very astute, but it's not going to get you anywhere," Binder cackled viciously.

"Why the girl? Why did you have to involve her?" Moore asked as he continued to probe for answers and buy time.

"She was an unexpected twist to our plans. She saw us kill Dedmon. We couldn't risk her going to the police and reporting us. She left us with no choice," Binder said with a malevolent stare.

"So you were going to kill her no matter what?"

"As if I had a choice?" Binder asked with cold emotional indifference. "We're wasting time. There is something you can do for me."

"What?"

"Drop to the floor. Pull back the rug you're standing on. You'll find several loose boards. I want you to pry them up," Binder instructed carefully.

Moore slowly did as he was ordered. The boards came away easily as Binder stood over Moore.

"Shine your light down the opening. It's only about a foot deep. Give me the sack that is down there."

Moore reached into the opening and carefully felt around. His hands contacted a damp, 2-ply cotton canvas sack. He grabbed it and lifted it slowly.

"This is all you found?" Moore scoffed ironically as he heard the coins clink together in the sack. It wasn't a quarter-full.

Pretending that it didn't bother him, Binder answered nonchalantly, "That's how it goes some time. Apparently, someone else found the treasure before me. That's all that was left."

"What a shame!" Moore exclaimed. "And two deaths – Dedmon and Carlson because of your greed." Moore didn't mention the third dead man in the chair near to him.

Anger flared in Binders eyes as he barked, "Hand me the sack!"

Moore had been busy opening the sack during their verbal exchange. He kept a grip on the bottom of the sack as he threw the open top end toward Binder, allowing the gold coins to fly through the air and scatter on the floor. While distracting Binder for a moment as he looked at the scattered coins, Moore launched himself through the air at Binder, striking a painful blow to his solar plexus in the center of his chest.

Binder screamed as he dropped his shotgun and the two fell to the floor as they grappled. Binder was able to work his way free of Moore's grasp and bounced to his feet. He withdrew a pistol from his waistband and aimed it at Moore who was on the floor looking up at Binder. Moore's clip-on cap headlamp lit up Binder's face.

Suddenly, a tapping on the front window caused Binder to freeze. It was Ashley, who then fired his AR-15 through the window as Moore flicked off his head lamp and rolled to the far side of the room. Binder yelled as Ashley's bullet grazed his side. He began firing blindly in the darkened room, trying to kill Moore.

The front door kicked open. Ashley then fired on automatic toward the spot where Binder had been standing but failed to bring him down. Binder escaped into the kitchen and out the back door.

Moore bounded to his feet. "Where in the world have you been?" Moore asked, slightly frustrated by how long it took Ashley to arrive.

"I was busy."

"What?" Moore asked with disbelief.

"You'll see," Ashley said with a confident grin as the two men ran into the kitchen. They heard the SUV door slam, and its engine accelerate, signaling that Binder was driving away.

"We're going to lose him," Moore cried as they burst through the kitchen door into the drizzling rain.

"I don't think so."

They next heard a crash as the speeding SUV lost control turning out of the driveway, crashing into a large live oak tree.

"I cut the brake line," Ashley grinned. "Just in case, you know?"

Moore started laughing. "Leave it to you. Ryan, you're incorrigible!"

The two men raced down the driveway where they found Binder emerging from the wrecked SUV.

"I'd drop that weapon," Moore demanded when he saw the handgun in Binder's hand. Instead, Binder brought the gun up to fire on the two men. It was a mistake as they both fired on him, killing him instantly.

Within minutes, three Southport police cars arrived, and Moore and Ashley found themselves explaining what had transpired. As expected, the police weren't pleased by the two men going after Binder. They had their hands slapped for not notifying law enforcement. After an hour of giving statements, they were on their way back to the marina, then home to Shallotte Point.

CHAPTER 22

Swanson's House
Shallotte Point

It was a sunny, late morning that included a gentle breeze sweeping across the riverbank in front of Swanson's house. The rustling leaves of a nearby live oak tree shaded the grass between the house and dock where Swanson's boat rocked quietly in the outgoing tide. Moore and Ashley finished recounting for Swanson and Neville their exciting adventure from the previous night in tracking down Binder in Southport, much to Swanson's delight.

"That just makes my day; ya catching that kidnapper and snuffing the life out of him!" Swanson smiled from his rocker.

"Let alone how rescuing that Chloe helped restore our friendship. We're best friends again, right Swaney?" Neville spoke in a pleasant tone from the other rocker on the porch.

Swanson was very pleased that the two men had buried the hatchet between them after all of those years, but he wasn't quite ready to start singing a duet with Neville. He knew that it would take more time for them to be as close as they once were.

"Ah, ain't ya the one with purty words?" Swanson suggested in a sarcastic tone.

"It's nothing," Neville smiled appreciatively.

"I guess ya can say that. Friends only give ya a shoulder to cry on." Swanson's eyes had a twinkle in them as he continued. "But best friends are ready with a shovel to knock some sense into ya," he guffawed.

Moore, Ashley and Dottie, who had been standing in front of the porch, joined in the laughter.

Moore's phone rang. It was Wilbanks.

"I'll be right back. I need to take this call from Ralph," Moore said as he walked around the corner of the house.

"Hi Ralph."

"Hello Emerson. I got y'all's phone message about the gold coins y'all found in Southport. Y'all are sure it's from the *Myrtle*?"

"That's what we think, but let me give you an update on what happened in the last 23 hours." Moore filled him in on what had occurred.

When Moore finished, Anne spoke, "Hey Emerson. It's Anne. Ralph had you on speakerphone. It sounds like you've been busier than a cat at a laser show."

"Oh my. You've been with Ralph too long. You're even starting to sound like him," Moore groaned.

"As long as I don't start looking like him," she joked.

"That, my sweetie pie, will never happen. But she's right. Y'all been busy. I'm glad that everything turned out okay for y'all, and that Chloe is safe," Wilbanks said.

"I'll get those coins to you so that you can take a look at them before you turn them in to the government."

"I'd love to see them." Wilbanks paused. "There's a reason for my call. There's something amiss, Emerson. I just feel it."

"How's that, Ralph?"

"I don't quite know. It's staring me in the face. Something I saw that is the missing piece to the puzzle. It's been bothering me since we got back home, and I started looking at the videos of the *Myrtle*."

Moore thought for a moment. "I don't have a clue as to how I can help you."

"Give me some time. I'll figure it out and let y'all know."

They ended their call and Moore returned to the riverfront side of the house. He found everyone standing by the dock where they were watching Chloe, Holden and Flynn boating on the river. Moore quickly joined them and stood next to Dottie.

"Anything important?" Ashley asked.

"I just updated Ralph on what's been happening," Moore explained as Dottie eased herself closer to Moore. He looked at her and the two exchanged warm smiles.

"It looks like the kids are having fun out there," Dottie spoke as they watched the trio on the river.

"I don't like it," Swanson grumbled. "That shipwreck has another hole in it. Ya watch now and ya will see them start bailing any minute," he warned.

"Maybe we should have junked that boat Swaney," Ashley suggested.

"I wouldn't go out on it, I'm telling ya," Swanson fussed. "Look now. Just like I said."

They all turned to see the trio in the boat start bailing water out. Holden had a small bucket while the other two were using their cupped hands. The water had begun to seep in a few minutes earlier, then the amount of water coming in through a widening crack in the boat bottom increased.

"Take us to shore," Holden called to Flynn urgently.

Flynn tried to start the motor, but it wouldn't start. Everything seemed to be failing at that moment. To make matters worse, Swanson's dog which had been standing next to Swanson began barking as loud as he could. Terrified, his fur stood on end as his frantic, high-pitched barks signaled approaching danger.

Swanson's eyes swept the river. "There's the reason little Shrimphead is so upset."

They all looked and saw what the dog and Swanson had spotted. An alligator was swimming downriver toward the sinking boat as it had been lurking nearby.

"Leatherhead sees a meal," he stormed angrily as he raced to his docked boat. "Who's coming with me?" he shouted as he jumped aboard his boat.

Neville, Ashley and Moore climbed aboard and released the lines as Swanson started its motor. Within seconds the boat was racing away from the dock toward the sinking boat.

"I'll get Barry and Corbett to help," Dottie shouted at the departing rescue boat.

"Thanks Dottie," Moore called back to her as she ran to the Holden Seafood Company building.

The trio in the sinking boat spotted the approaching alligator and Chloe began to frantically scream. The incoming water from the boat bottom was pouring in faster as the crack widened. The sides of the craft were sinking lower and lower in the river. Swanson pushed forward on the throttle as he headed his boat to the far side of the river.

"Be calm," Swanson called.

"We'll be there in a second," Neville yelled from the bow.

The faces of the panicked teens were filled with fear as the alligator nudged against the boat. His long jaws opened, showing its sharp row of teeth.

Snapping at them, its body surged out of the river at the boat, almost causing the boat to tip over. The teens threw their weight against the other side of the boat in an attempt to counterbalance the gator's weight. Fortunately, not enough of the gator's body had rocketed out of the river.

Nearing the sinking craft, Swanson slowed his boat, reversing its motor as he swung the bow in a turn to bring it close to

Flynn's boat.

"Chloe, jump over here" Moore ordered as he held out his arms.

The distraught teen looked at the distance between the two boats and froze. She was terrified as she heard the gator trying again to climb aboard Flynn's boat. The gator's actions threatened again to tip over the boat.

"Jump, Chloe!" Ashley called, trying to encourage his sister.

Terror-stricken, she tried to put aside her fear as she jumped the three feet across the open water into Moore's waiting arms. Moore passed her to Ashley who held the sobbing teen close. "It's okay. You're safe now," he said as he comforted her.

Meanwhile, Swanson was keeping enough speed on the boat to stay even with Flynn's boat as the two headed with the tide down river.

"Come on Holden! Jump!" Moore called as Holden hit the gator on the head with an oar.

"No. I'll stay here. Archie, you go first," Holden yelled as he walloped the gator another time, making the gator angrier.

Flynn took one last look at Holden, then jumped into the outstretched arms of Moore and Neville. Flynn's boat was filling fast. The gunwales were disappearing below the river surface as the gator slipped back into the river. Holden splashed his way across the rapidly sinking boat, preparing to jump.

"Jump!" Moore called.

Holden started to jump, but his wet feet slipped out from under him. He began to fall into the river, but Moore and Neville leaned over precariously to grab his arms. He was waist-deep in the water as the boat sunk. As they pulled him up, Neville lost his balance and plummeted in the river. He disappeared from sight as the gator submerged.

"Neville's in the river. The gator is after him!" Moore called to Swanson.

"Take the helm, Ryan!" Swanson yelled as Ashley quickly moved to the wheel. Grabbing his knife from its sheath, Swanson took five steps to the edge of the boat. "This is becoming a headache," he roared as he dove into the river.

The gator and Neville surfaced downriver. The gator was shaking a screaming Neville like a rag doll as it clamped down on his arm. Blood was gushing from the deep wounds. He was reaching around with his free hand, trying to break loose by poking the gator in the eye.

Swanson swam with powerful strokes that took him quickly to Neville's side. The three disappeared under the water amidst the gator's thrashing movements. While Flynn's boat sank, Ashley maneuvered Swanson's boat to a spot near where the two men and gator were last sighted.

Neville's head broke the surface. "Help! Help!" he yelled frantically.

"We're coming!" Ashley shouted as he moved the boat next to Neville. Moore, Holden and Flynn reached over to pull him aboard, being careful how they handled his bleeding left arm.

"Is there anything here to stop the bleeding?" Moore asked as he looked around the boat.

"Take my sweater," Chloe offered as she shucked the cotton sweater, and Moore used it to wrap it tightly around the wound.

"Holden. Keep a tight hold on this," Moore said as he turned his attention back to the river, searching for Swanson.

"There!" Flynn yelled, pointing farther downriver where the thrashing and twisting gator surfaced as Swanson wrestled with it. Just as quickly, they submerged again and the frothing in the water stopped.

The anxious group on board Swanson's boat became uncomfortable as an eerie silence filled the air. Two minutes passed before the gator surfaced. Swanson's knife protruded from the scaly skin covering the gator's head. The knife was imbedded deeply into its brain.

"He got him!" Flynn yelled excitedly as they all felt some sense of relief.

"Swaney! Swaney!" they all began to call as they anxiously scanned the river's surface. But as much as they called and looked, they were greeted by silence as Ashley held the boat in position.

"Ain't nobody that can stay under that long," Neville stated as a somber mood descended on the group. "He's dead," Neville said gloomily.

With tears in his eyes, Holden was the first to speak. "You're alive Neville because my grandad jumped in to save you. You realize that, right?"

"I do. I'm grateful. I'm just glad that we had a chance to forgive each other and make up a bit," Neville moaned. "He was a legend in these parts."

Flynn moved next to Holden, placing his arm on his shoulder. "I'm so sorry about you losing your grandad, Holden. They don't make them like him anymore."

"Thanks Archie."

"He was a sweet man, Holden," Chloe commented sadly as she placed her arm around Holden.

"A character like no other. He epitomized a tough seagoing trawler captain," Ashley commented as his eyes scanned the river for any sign of Swanson's body.

"A legend," Moore added as a black cloud of grief settled over the group. They stood in silence as they all hoped Swanson would reappear.

"Is that him?" Chloe asked when she saw a dark object come into view.

As it floated by them, Flynn answered, "It's a tree log."

"Oh," a disappointed Chloe responded.

"Doesn't anyone else have anything good to say about that old cuss? What's wrong with ya? Run out of words?" a familiar voice boomed from the other side of the boat.

They all turned to see Swanson's head peering up at them as his hand gripped the side of the boat. His face was covered with a mischievous grin.

"News of my death is premature, but I did enjoy hearing all the nice stuff ya was saying about me. Ya need more practice though for when my real demise rolls around. Now somebody come over here and help me haul my sorry butt out of this river. I'm plumb tired out. It's not like I make a daily habit out of hand-to-hand combat with a gator," he cackled.

"Swaney! We thought you were dead!" came the shouts of glee from the boat occupants at seeing the ornery trawler captain.

"Quit yer jawing and help me up," he shouted as he struggled to pull himself out of the river.

Ashley and Moore reached over the side and grabbed his outstretched arms, pulling him on board. Swanson sat and took several deep breaths.

"Where's my gator? I'm going to have a pair of cowboy boots made out of him," Swanson said as he looked around the river.

"It's floating downriver, but we can fetch it," Ashley said as he engaged the throttle and moved the craft to catch up with the floating gator.

Swanson turned his head to stare at Neville. "Are ya okay?"

Neville held up his bandaged arm. "Just a scratch," he answered as he minimized the damage.

"Like I told ya before, don't go and make this rescuing Neville stuff a habit. Yer wearing me out, Neville," Swanson stated half-seriously.

"We were really worried about you, Swaney," Moore said as he expressed his concern.

"Ya don't need to be. Besides, I was taking care of business," Swanson retorted.

"Taking care of business?" Moore asked perplexed.

"That's right. I was visiting the First Bank of Swanson," he smiled as he reached into his pocket with his right hand. When he withdrew it, he was holding several gold coins.

"Where did you get those?" Moore stammered in surprise.

Swanson leaned back. "I guess it don't matter now if I tell ya all what I've been up to many nights."

"Your boat in the river?" Moore questioned.

"That's right. My grandad used to tell me tales about sunken Confederate ships when I was a kid. Ya know several were found off the end of Holden Island, right?"

They all nodded.

"My grandad would hear rumors about a ghost ship. It was supposed to carry a load of gold coins, but it was lost. I think the ghost ship was that *Myrtle* ya all found off the island."

"That was off the island, not here in the river," Moore remarked with a questioning look on his face. "Did you find the gold and move it here in the river for safekeeping?" Moore probed.

"Not me, but somebody did," Swanson surmised. "If a storm blew up, ya'd want to make sure a cargo of that nature would be safe, right?"

They all nodded again.

"There's the gator," Ashley interrupted their conversation as he eased the boat next to the carcass.

"Holden, take a line and tie one end to that gator. We'll tow it back to the dock," Swanson instructed.

Holden bent to the task, and in a few minutes the boat with the gator in tow was headed back to Swanson's dock.

Moore had an idea. "Before you continue, Swaney, let me make a phone call."

"Call whoever ya want except the folks at the Internal Revenue Service," Swanson cracked.

Moore called Wilbanks. The call was answered on the first ring.

"Hello Emerson. I was just thinking about y'all."

"Good. I've got a question for you. Did you notice how many skiffs were aboard the *Myrtle*?"

"I do believe y'all are reading my mind. That's why I was thinking of giving y'all a call. Remember I said there was something bugging me like the piece of a missing puzzle?"

"Yes."

"Well here it is. I studied the videos of the shipwreck closely. There was a skiff missing. That means it may have been launched before the storm with the treasure to take it to safekeeping."

Moore beamed. "That's great news."

"Hang on there. What would y'all say if I told y'all that I had better news?"

"I'm waiting."

"I focused in on the remaining skiffs on that shipwreck. I should say the oars. I saw one of the oars when I was there visiting y'all."

"Where was that?"

"In Swaney's house. It's on the wall. I knew that I had seen something somewhere it didn't belong and that was it."

Moore looked at Swanson. Swanson shrugged his shoulders as he sheepishly grinned back.

"Thanks, Ralph. That's the missing puzzle piece. I'll get back to you," Moore said as he ended the call. Moore turned to Swanson. "You want to tell us what you've been holding back?"

"I guess I'm caught with my pants down. Oops. Sorry Chloe. I should have said something else."

Chloe flashed a brief smile at Swanson.

"Well, I did hold back a bit of the story. My grandad's father found that oar washed up after a big storm in the marsh grass. He also found the corpse of a Confederate sailor nearby. He buried him.

"He wondered what they both would be doing up the river so far unless they were escaping that storm. Nobody knew that a ship went down or that it might have been carrying gold coins. The story has been passed down for generations. I was the only one to start looking for the sunken skiff. I've always wanted to find treasure. After I retired, I had extra time to work the river."

"Why do it at night?" Moore asked.

"It would cause too much of a commotion. Better for folk around here to think I was an old, crazy guy," Swanson explained.

"They do!" Flynn chipped in.

Swanson laughed. "Ya can guess that I didn't find anything until today. When I was killing that gator, I got snagged on a piece of timber."

"You were underwater for a long time," Moore observed.

"I'm pretty good at holding my breath," Swanson said before he continued. "I got free of it and followed it down to a skiff sunk in the river mud. I looked around and figured that it was the one I had heard about. Then I saw some bags. When I grabbed one, it ripped open from the weight. It was full of gold coins. I grabbed a handful to bring up with me."

As he concluded his story, Ashley nudged the boat against Swanson's dock where Dottie, Barry, Corbett and Roddy were waiting.

"I'm so glad you all are safe," Dottie offered as Chloe stepped off the boat and into Dottie's arms.

"Looks like you got old Leatherhead, Swaney" Barry remarked as he saw the dead gator behind the boat.

"It was a battle, but I'm going to get that pair of alligator cowboy boots I've always wanted," Swanson commented with a grin.

"Swaney found some gold coins," Chloe exclaimed excitedly.

"Yes, he did. Grandad found gold coins, Mom," Holden chimed in.

Dottie turned to Swanson as did the other new arrivals. "Is that true, Dad?"

"I found a handful," he admitted slowly. He then retold the tale he had shared in the boat with the others.

"Remember Grandad, I promised you that you'd find what you were looking for," Holden beamed.

"That's right Holden. It was always Holden's promise," Swanson smiled.

"Isn't that awesome!" Ashley whooped with excitement.

"There's more down there," Moore added.

CHAPTER 23

**Two Days Later
Shallotte Point**

The prior 48 hours had been a busy time at Shallotte Point. Moore had not only called Wilbanks to let him know about the discovery of the coins, but he also wrote a story for *The Washington Post* about Binder, the *Myrtle*, Chloe's kidnapping and rescue, and the gold coin discovery. He had emailed the story to his editor John Sedler, who was now talking to Moore by phone.

"Good story, Emerson, but it doesn't sound like you did much relaxing on this beach vacation trip," Sedler's deep voice noted.

"When do I ever?" Moore asked as he sat on Ashley's front porch.

"I'm going to make some edits to it, and we'll publish it in tomorrow's edition."

"Great. John?" Moore asked as he watched Dottie drive up to Swanson's house and park. He watched as the beautiful woman stepped out of the car and walked toward the house.

"Yes, although I think I know what's coming," Sedler replied with a soft chuckle.

"Since this turned out to be a working vacation, I'd like to spend a few more days here to relax. Any problem with that?" Moore asked, anxious to end the call and head to Swanson's house.

"How many days?"

"That depends," Moore answered as he thought it could end up being a very long stay.

"On?"

Moore knew that Sedler wouldn't stop until he gave him a straight answer. "On a certain blonde."

Sedler snickered. "Methinks romance is in the air."

"It could very well be," Moore admitted.

"Go on and stay awhile longer. But one thing, Emerson."

Moore heard the cautionary tone in Sedler's voice. "What's that?"

"Please don't get involved in another adventure. Just relax."

Moore laughed. "That's my plan," he said as they ended the call.

Ashley walked onto the porch.

"Ryan, is it okay if I stay here a few more days?"

"Sure. Stay as long as you like. Rachel and I like having you around."

"Great. Thank you. I'm going over to see Swaney," Moore said as he walked out of the enclosed porch.

Ashley didn't comment. He had already noticed that Dottie was visiting her father, too. Moore quickly crossed the space between the houses to Swanson's. Seeing him approach, Dottie greeted him warmly. "Hello Emerson. It's a beautiful day."

"Even more so when you're here to brighten it up," Moore flirted.

In response to the comment, Moore heard someone coughing loud from the porch to get Moore's attention. It was Swanson.

"That flirting is a risky game, Emerson," Swanson warned as he pet his Yorkie. "Isn't that right, Shrimphead?"

The dog barked twice in response.

"How's that, Swaney?"

"One mistake and you're committed," he guffawed.

"Dad!" Dottie teased.

"I was just saying."

Moore turned his attention to the activity on the river. There were two boats from the North Carolina state government at anchor. Two dive teams were busy bringing up the gold coins.

"Didn't take long for them to get involved," Moore observed.

"Government people. They're taking ownership of all them gold coins," Swanson roared.

"That's a shame, Dad," Dottie said remorsefully. "They didn't let you keep any of the coins?"

"Nah. Ya know the government. They get it all," he stated full of frustration.

Moore noticed the hide of the alligator hanging from the live oak. "You didn't waste any time in skinning that gator."

"Nope. I told ya I was going to get me a pair of gator cowboy boots. Step #1 complete," he smiled.

The sound of an approaching boat caught their attention. It was Neville. He brought the boat around and docked it next to Swanson's boat.

"I like your new boat," Moore said as Neville walked up to the house.

"So do I," Neville said with a huge grin. "You know that my old one sunk, right?"

"Yes," Moore agreed.

Their conversation was interrupted by a shout from the river. Coming downriver were Flynn, Holden and Chloe in a new boat.

"How do you like my new boat?" Flynn called from the helm to Moore.

Moore's eyebrows raised as he started putting two and two

together. He looked at Swanson who gave him a wink.

"It looks nice!" Moore called.

"And seaworthy," Swanson duly noted with a sly smile.

"We're going to Holden Beach for the day. Anyone want to come with us?" Chloe shouted.

"No. You all have a fun time and be careful," Dottie hollered.

"Hey Mom! Grandad's buying me a boat tomorrow. We're going to Wilmington to look at several," Holden yelled happily.

"That's nice," she commented as the boat moved downriver. "Dad, what are you doing?"

"I just figure that life's too short, and I should be doing some nice things for some people. But don't ya tell anybody. I don't want people to think I'm going soft, ya know."

"Or that someone may have been on the river two nights ago to harvest some of those gold coins before the state people showed up," Moore uttered quietly.

"Ya saw me?" Swanson asked as his head whipped around to look at Moore.

Moore nodded his head.

Swanson's face changed to a serious look. "Now, don't any of ya breathe a word about that to anyone. Those government boys out there aren't going to miss a few coins. They don't even know how many were there to start with," he smiled mischievously. "Are ya with me?"

They all nodded except Neville who spoke. "I am and thank you for the new boat."

"Since I was responsible for ya losing the other one, I thought it would be the right thing to do."

Moore turned to Dottie. "Would you like to join me for lunch at the Flounder Pier? Ryan said I could use his boat today."

"I'd be delighted."

They bid farewell to Swanson and Neville, then walked over to the dock at the Holden Seafood Company. Moore stepped aboard Ashley's boat, then reached for Dottie's hand to assist her on board. When she got aboard, Moore pulled her in close.

"I'm planning on taking some serious time off," he said as he looked deep into her eyes.

"I was kind of hoping that you'd stay here for a while," she agreed as her coral blue eyes radiated with a sweet tenderness.

He leaned toward her, bringing them even closer to each other. Her lips in a casual, silent way were inviting as their heads closed. They locked lips in a burst of intoxicating passion.

COMING SOON
Next *George Ivers* Adventure:
Alone at Home

About the Author
Bob Adamov

Bob Adamov is an award-winning, Ohio mystery adventure author whose stories are based in the Lake Erie South Bass Island resort village of Put-in-Bay, the "Key West of the Midwest." His novels, with the exception of *Memory Layne*, follow the adventures of investigative reporter Emerson Moore, and are written in the style of Adamov's favorite author, Clive Cussler.

Adamov was the featured author at the 2006 Ernest Hemingway Days' Literary Festival in Key West and named Writer of the Year by the University of Akron's Wayne College in 2010. Adamov has also presented for several of the Clive Cussler Collectors' Society conventions.

A graduate of Kent State University, Adamov resides in Wooster, Ohio. He can often be seen in Put-in-Bay, Key West, Chincoteague, North Carolina's Brunswick Islands and the Cayman Islands with his scuba diving and treasure hunting friends. Previously, he worked for an Arlington, Virginia-based defense contractor in the intelligence sector.

Adamov celebrated the release of his first novel *Rainbow's End* 20 years ago on October 19, 2022 with a rewritten 20th anniversary edition. He is working on his 20th novel, *Alone at Home*.

© 2024 Packard Island Publishing
www.packardislandpublishing.com

Printed in the USA
CPSIA information can be obtained
at www.ICGtesting.com
CBHW022251271124
18131CB00010B/51